DEATH IN THE SKIES

The flaming ship was now pitifully straining for altitude, left wing held high as if to save it from the inferno. The big ones die hard, I thought. Then this one died. At the top of the wingover, the doomed B-24 gave up. It didn't blow; it just melted apart. Like a bird caught by a blast of shot, the heavy parts fell first, the feathers of debris followed in a long string of smoking wreckage. Out of the feathers, a parachute took form.

Then blue sky returned. An empty, beautiful blue. Empty of a great bomber and ten men. Just like that.

We had finally found our war.

ELUSIVE HORIZONS

KEITH C. SCHUYLER

AVON BOOKS ◆ NEW YORK

All poetry excerpts are from original and unpublished work of the author.

AVON BOOKS
A division of
The Hearst Corporation
1350 Avenue of the Americas
New York, New York 10019

First Avon Books Printing: January 1992

AVON TRADEMARK REG. U.S. PAT. OFF. AND IN OTHER COUNTRIES, MARCA REGISTRADA, HECHO EN U.S.A.

Printed in the U.S.A.

RA   10   9   8   7   6   5   4   3   2   1

*Dedicated to nine men
and the B-24*

Preface

There are a number of ways to write a story. In *fiction*, the author can make his characters perform according to his wishes. In *fact*, a series of events can be glamorized to make a hero of anybody who comes to public attention. In the autobiographical paragraph which follows, from the stuck-together pages of World War II, only the raw truth is presented.

It took the writer nearly a quarter of a century to find the courage to bare the soul of the youngster he was when all this happened. The unheroic events which involved me and my crew were so routine, and so typical of so many, that this in itself becomes the story. I have tried to speak for the other unheroes so that you might know some of what happened behind the headlines.

This book, was, nevertheless, deliberate. I started planning before we left the States. The events were written down within hours of their happening. They are the truth as I recorded it and as I remembered it.

We were the lucky ones. Despite the fear, the mistakes, the frustrations, the terror, we did finally return. But we saw something of the really great stories that blew up in a flash of dirty red flame, sank beneath the chill waters of the North Sea or smashed into the bloodsoaked mountains and meadows of the European continent.

But, we, too, tried. My God, how we tried. And our

effort was tied to the wing of one of the greatest airplanes
that ever lived—the B-24 Liberator Bomber.

KEITH C. SCHUYLER

1

Elusive horizons, retreating lines,
  That divide the Now, from Soon or Never,
  Calling vagrant spirits onward ever.
Strong ferment to adventure's heady wines,
  Of which we do not sanely sip, but drink
  Great thirsty draughts, and in our pleasure think
    Not of those horizons that mark our waiting shrines.

We gain horizons boiling in the sun;
  We conquer where they dance upon the sands
  Or trace the face of mountains in strange lands
Afar. We seek them when the day is done
  And pass them in the night; o'er moor and lea;
  To where they press the sky back from the sea.
    And, we may some day search beyond them all—
    but one.

But one—That we ever have our eyes on
  Hopefully, fearfully, when thoughts turn face
  From life on earth; for that great hallowed space
Across the line, which fate's finger lies on
  Sternly, holds back all puny earthly things.
  And yet, I pray to shed my silver wings
    One day and soar high beyond—the Last Horizon.

She was beautiful in action, I had to admit grudgingly, and some of her masters seemed to have a real affection for her. But to me she was a symbol of my own frustration.

And, I was afraid of her.

I hated her guts; the sight of her; I hated everything about this pot-bellied bitch of an airplane. But now she's gone, and I swallow a lump every time I hear one of the heavies going over. For, in between the time I came to hate and fear her and the time I jumped from her flaming bowels, I learned to love and to respect her with an almost passionate intensity.

Like a second vice-president with a broad back and a weak mind, the B-24 Liberator bomber has been denied her rightful glory. They should have used a wide-angle lens when they took the picture of the vaunted B-17 Flying Fortress in World War II. Because, sitting right beside her was a deep-keeled, narrow-winged witch of an airplane that could fly rings around the press agent's delight.

And yet, one of the unhappiest days of my life was that on which I was started toward my affair with the B-24. My case was a typical Army fluke.

All through aviation cadet training we had been issued forms on which we indicated our preference for combat planes. Every time I faithfully filled in "fighters" for each of the three choices allowed. By the time our class finished basic, my 201 file was loaded with these forms. And, when the day arrived for assignment to either twin-engine or single-engine advanced school, it was practically assured that I would be headed for AT-6's—last step in training before being assigned to P-51's or P-47's. I was. Orders were cut.

But, late the afternoon before we were to depart, a new order came out. It had been discovered that too many had been assigned to single-engine school, and twenty names would be deleted from the list. These names, the CO indicated, would be picked at random.

I was random.

With tears of rage clouding my vision, I made a frontal

attack on my squadron CO, one that would have earned me a washout under less extenuating circumstances.

"From the day I entered the army I wanted fighters," I practically screamed. "I've kept my nose clean, worked my guts out, did everything that was asked of me. I'm built for fighters; I'm too damned short for those big box cars and you know it!"

The CO looked down on my five-foot-seven, and was forced to agree.

"But you'll get to like them," he attempted lamely.

"Look"—I boiled—"I came into flying for one thing: to fly fighters. If I can't have them, send me to the infantry. I don't want to fly anything but fighters. I'm through."

It did no good. The CO gave me his sympathy, but he could do nothing toward getting the orders changed. There would always be the chance that I'd go on to twin-engine fighters, P-38's. Anyway, I'd be all right as soon as I got over my disappointment, he said. But my disappointment was still with me when I left Walnut Ridge, Arkansas, and headed in deep gloom to Freeman Field at Seymour, Indiana.

AT-10's, flying matchboxes they called them, were waiting for us. Somehow the dread of flying heavy bombers was lightened in the new interest provided by the flimsy twin-engine jobs. Anyway, there was still the hope of getting into twin-engine fighters. But my own capabilities, or lack of them, denied me whatever chance I might have had.

I found it in my 201 file long afterward. Two of my best flying grades were in night flying and formation flying. Unconsciously I was fanning the flames under my own kettle of imagined misfortune. They finally handed me a pair of wings, a ticket for Smyrna, Tennessee, and B-24 bombers.

This was the unkindest cut of all. If it *had* to be heavies, why couldn't it at least be B-17's! The Air Corps press agents had me taken in, too.

The hate I had developed for big airplanes squeezed over to admit fear the first time I looked at a Liberator on the ramp. They never were a pretty sight at best—those four huge engines tacked onto a slip of a wing, belly nearly dragging the concrete, and hog-nose stuck way too far forward. Even the olive-drab paint gave their skin a sickly color. And, like pregnant hippopotamuses, they bucked and snorted their way around the hangars, letting out an occasional squeak of rubber, their constant bloat seeming to substantiate the foul odors that drifted from them.

Only pride could have dragged me to the flight line for my first trip aloft in a B-24. I wanted no part of them. But the wings I wore had come hard. Keeping them would come harder. They took on new value when I ducked under the dirty-green belly and climbed fearfully to the flight deck.

First of the four Pratt-Whitneys wheezed, gargled great gobs of black cotton recklessly, and then sprang into thunder, harnessing more horses than all the planes I had flown to that moment. Four of them, 4800 war horses tugging at the skinny wing that seemed incapable of supporting its own tips. And, somehow, at the urging of the throttles, the wing moved, and with it the ponderous fuselage reluctantly kept pace.

That the thing would fly at all was of sufficient interest to arouse my momentary curiosity. The instructor, who had said little, transmitted a confidence that partially beat back my fear as the great ship waddled past the hangars, groaned around a corner, and tiptoed clumsily down a taxi strip that seemed too narrow to accommodate it.

Always before, I had felt some personal measure of confidence, even on the first dual instruction flight I had taken in the little Fairchild trainers back in primary school. Now, with two hundred hours of flying behind me, I sat numb and helpless as my instructor followed his check list and one by one wound up the Pratts to test them. The '24 shook and shuddered painfully, but the rpm needles and manifold pressure gauges read correctly, and everything else seemed satisfactory. The tower cleared us, and the stripped-down bomber shuffled into takeoff position.

My instructor nodded, pointed at the controls for me to

follow through. Gingerly I reached for the strange half-wheel and distant rudder pedals. I got the wheel all right, but only the tips of my flying boots touched the rudders! With my seat full forward I was still too short in the britches.

It didn't matter for the moment; nothing mattered, for the engines were in full-throated roar and we were moving. How even those engines could move the complicated mass of metal covered machinery was amazing enough, but that the thing actually left the runway when the stick came back was a real miracle to me. It would fly.

Yes, it would fly. How well I came to know it! Every day that the weather allowed I was jammed between the rudders and a pack of cushions, wrestling and bullying one of the big jobs under the tutelage of an instructor. Takeoffs and landings, takeoffs and landings. Instrument flights, cross-country flights. More takeoffs, more landings.

I particularly remember one day sitting beside a slender redhead with captain's bars after we had shot half a dozen landings in the hot sun. He was completely at ease, fresh as a daisy; I was wringing wet with perspiration, arms aching in every joint.

"How do you do it? How long does a fellow have to fly these things to take it the way you do?"

He grinned. "Oh, you get used to it," he replied with completely unaffected nonchalance.

Another day, when I wasn't sweating quite so much, I asked, "Don't you get awfully sick of flying these wrecks?"

He didn't grin this time; he actually looked offended.

"There's nothing wrong with these airplanes. After a while you get to like them."

The guy was serious!

"How many years does that take?"

My disgust and distrust was obvious. And when he answered, he spoke almost sympathetically, but with complete seriousness.

"Don't let them get you down, Lieutenant. I promise

you that you will learn to like the '24. She's actually a fine airplane.''

"How long does it really take?" This time the question was earnest. I *wanted* to like the ship. By this time I had given up all hope of getting into fighters.

"About seventy hours."

After that I tried harder.

It was one day while roaring down the runway that I suddenly came to realize that I was no longer afraid of the B-24. I kept her down longer than necessary, building up speed, and when I pulled her off the concrete, she lifted with a flourish and new life. When I wanted to turn, she turned . . . smooth coordinated banks that kept the seat of my pants tight against the bucket seat whether we were tipping ten degrees or seventy.

When I forced her into a stall, with every prop attempting to take its own direction, she broke cleanly. And when I brought her back to the strip, she whispered in, tires letting out only a little squeal of delight.

Maybe I was just feeling better than usual that time, but the next day I actually looked forward to getting back into the air. The instructor, another student, and I started just before dark on a cross-country to Charleston, South Carolina. I flew out and navigated back; hit Smyrna within one mile, using only the radio compass despite bad storms near our course that made the needle dance like a weed in a high wind. Those bombers *could* get around.

That flight brought my time in B-24's up to a *little over seventy hours*. The redhead was right.

With transition over, our gang moved on up to Casper, Wyoming, after a stop at Salt Lake City. We were given a lot more night flying and formation flying . . . night and day. Then, from all over the country, crews began pouring in to make up combat units.

My first co-pilot was a boy who had trained to be first pilot on a B-17. He was as sour on the idea as I had been when I went to Indiana to twin-engine school. But he was not half as disgruntled as members of a big group sent in from fresh out of single-engine advanced school—to be *co-pilots* on B-24's!

Fortunately, in a way, the lieutenant assigned to me was later given his own crew. His substitute was a big, good-looking kid fresh out of twin-engine advanced school. I say "in a way" because my first man was later killed in combat. The inexperienced replacements came in shortly before we were ready to leave for overseas.

By this time, the B-24 had become as much a part of me as my slightly tarnished gold bars. Anyone who escaped a winter in Casper and the 80-mph winds that whipped man and plane relentlessly had to join with their ship or die with it on the rugged mountains over which we flew, and flew and flew. Old airplanes and poor maintenance doubled the risk.

We lived through: one landing with the nose wheel cocked at 45 degrees and half the personnel of the field lined up along the hangars with morbid expectancy; a return trip through the night with gas streaming from a defective cap; a runaway prop that forced a three-engine takeoff; an engine cutout when we were scraping sand on an air-to-ground gunnery run; a shot-up vertical stabilizer when a flexible waist gun escaped its restrictor cables and peppered our tail.

In the battle of Casper, there developed between me and the B-24 an affinity born of necessity. When all her hundred-odd instruments and her four engines functioned properly, she took the initiative and carried us where we wanted to go and in the manner to which we had become accustomed. When things went wrong, the old girl depended upon me to get her back.

I had been told that there was no feel to the Liberator. That she was strictly an instrument ship, a mechanical monster that answered with robot obedience to any command. Nothing could have been further from reality.

Like any airplane, she was a flying machine, and God bless the men who made her. There never will be an airplane without feel or without feelings. There will never be a pilot who can fly without becoming a part of that airplane and who can share those feelings.

We flew to Europe in one fresh off the assembly line. They told our crew often that she was ours, and never did an airplane have more affection bestowed upon it. Down from Florida to Brazil, across the South Atlantic to Africa and up to Wales we went with her, and we babied her all the way.

I'll always remember that ship, 29511, because I named her after my wife, *Sweet Eloise*. And, I paid a GI seven bucks in Marraketch to paint the name along her nose. It was just before our last hop to Wales. If anyone knows what happened to her, I'd like to know.* For the moment we set foot on ground again, they took her from us.

We were just a replacement crew.

Late winter and early spring was a tough time in 1944 for bomber crews—especially replacement crews. The only good airplanes were those ferried over by replacements and they went to the old crews who were most apt to get the most good out of them. The battle-damaged wrecks that were left went to the green crews.

On the field of the 44th Bomb Group, oldest B-24 outfit in England, the plane supply was at an especially low ebb. Many of those remaining were in sad shape, war-weary and battle-scarred. New planes and new crews were needed badly.

Some of the new '24's we had ferried were already in use by the time our gang piled off the trucks at the site of

---

* After trying for years to trace what became of *Sweet Eloise*, in January, 1991, her history was revealed by Thomas Brittan of Kent, England, who makes a hobby of recording the history of all American and British planes that flew out of England in World War II. After I left her at Wales, she was assigned to the 392nd Bomb Group at Wendling to replace a 567th Squadron aircraft lost in March. In August, she went to the 579th Squadron, and after nose wheel repairs in October, was assigned to the 578th Squadron. She was returned to the U.S. in June, 1945, believed to have completed 150 missions.

the 44th. We represented ten brand-new complete bomber crews: forty officers and sixty noncoms. But none of us was destined to get many flights in *new* airplanes for a long time to come.

2

You can take your choice of chances
Amid the scourge of man-made ills
Where foul Satan's hand enhances
The bloody thirst for lethal thrills.
There's no end to hell and horror;
There's no dearth of dreadful dying;
Along Thor's gruesome corridor
Where the darts of death are flying.
From "A Pilot's Plea"

The first B-24 Liberator bomber took off from Lindbergh Field, adjacent to Consolidated Vultee Aircraft Corporation's San Diego plant on December 29, 1939. Born out of necessity to give the United States a second bomber to augment the B-17 Flying Fortress, the Liberator was spawned on the drawing board just nine months before she took to the air in San Diego. Possibly it takes exactly this time to impart human qualities to anything. For, the B-24 was built to carry ten souls inside her thin skin, and her character ran the gamut of female unpredictability, cantankerousness, and forgiveness.

When she stretched her 110-foot wings, she was the biggest thing we had to offer at the time. Her four 1200 hp Pratt & Whitney supercharged plants would drag her along at about 180 indicated statute miles per hour, which was something over 200 above 10,000 feet, depending upon the age of her engines and the accuracy of the air speed indicator. She was advertised at a cruising speed of 230 mph at 25,000 feet. The best I ever did was 30,000 feet in a stripped-down, beat-up, war-weary beast that we used for training in the States. It was *said* she would go up to 56,000 feet.

Her listed weight of 36,000 pounds empty was probably right, but her published gross weight of *over* 56,000 pounds was worth little more than a smile. I weighed 60,000 pounds taking off from Morrison Field at West Palm Beach in Florida with a load of homing pigeons, mail, assorted airplane parts, us, and all the gasoline they could jam into her—just starting out for war!

It was also said that she could carry ten tons on a short haul. We found that four tons was a big load to get off from the fields in England.

But, whatever the advertisements, the B-24 was the best thing available in 1944. Prime Minister Winston Churchill trusted her to get him to Russia and Africa—and back. And, some of our generals made plush airliners out of her.

Despite what was said about the B-17 which came first, and the B-29 which followed the B-24, more Liberators were used in World War II than any other type of four-engine bomber. About 18,000 of them were built, and they dropped 634,831 tons of bombs on 312,734 sorties. A total of 4,189 enemy aircraft fell to the ten .50-caliber machine guns they carried as armament.

Just a bit over half as long as she was wide, the Liberator measured 66 feet, 4 inches from nose turret to tail turret. And, with her nose wheel on the ground, crews had to climb 18 feet to service her topside. In all, her general measurements left something to be desired in the feminine line, but she was all lady in the air.

After losing the only new bomber we had ever flown, the one that had been given to us in Topeka, Kansas, it was quite a letdown to see what was offered on the base of the 44th Bomb Group. One of a cluster of airfields in

England's East Anglia, our concrete pasture was located near the village of Shipdham, not far from Norwich, in Norfolk County, south of The Wash. The base was an ugly sprawl of Nissen huts and stucco buildings with airplanes to match.

The 44th had staggered up from Africa after being mauled at Ploesti and a few other choice targets. It had literally been wiped out several times over when numbers of planes lost were compared to the normal complement on the field. It was putting aloft about thirty-six planes to a mission when we arrived. Four didn't make it back that day. It was early March, 1944.

They were glad to see us at the 44th, I guess. At least the CO of the 66th Bomb Squadron to which my crew was assigned seemed glad to see us. But we were a long way from combat despite an attack by the Germans somewhere south of us that first night on the field.

As we entered the Nissen hut reserved for us, we wondered about the empty cots so stark in the damp coldness. The sergeant who greeted us turned back to the chest of drawers he was emptying.

"Here, Lieutenant. You might as well have this."

I caught the half-empty bottle and saw that it was aftershave lotion. Again the sergeant turned, several packs of cigarettes in his hand.

"There is no point in sending stuff like this back," he explained half-apologetically. "If you don't take it, the vultures over at headquarters will get it." He turned back to the chest, picked off a picture of a girl, glanced briefly at it, then dropped it into a large bag. "I'll be out of here in a minute."

Larry, Dale, Jack, and I exchanged glances. None of us knew who had been in the hut before. But suddenly it seemed much larger and much more empty. The same thought made the rounds. Would someone be collecting soon to send our belongings back to the United States—a pitiful pile of secondhand hairbrushes, underwear, souvenirs, and maybe a few short snorter bills picked up on the way over—as evidence that we, too, fought the war in Europe?

A replacement crew was a lonely entity. It was accepted to take over a spot which might have belonged to one of the old gang who had earned a certain affection and respect. Either the old crew was on the way home, rotting in prison camps, or scattered in charred chunks of flesh and bone somewhere east. In any event, it had left a void that no replacement crew could possibly deserve until it earned it. Unless, of course, the missing crew was also a new replacement. In that case, it wouldn't be particularly missed except by people like the girl behind the picture that went so unceremoniously into the bag. There were only a few men on the base of the 44th Bomb Group who had completed their twenty-five missions to earn an overseas pass to home.

"Well, where do we go from here?" Jack broke the uncomfortable stillness as we started to sort out our belongings. It was more an expression than a question, but an answer came from an unexpected source.

"You Macs will see plenty of action. Just take it from old Mac."

The announcement came from an armload of wood staggering through the door ahead of a Latin type topped by a shock of curly black hair. As the wood tumbled in a heap beside the potbellied stove, somewhat swarthy features revealed themselves behind a nose that wandered decisively to the left. "There's a lot of war left. I'm Mac." He offered his hand around our little circle of officers.

"You just gotta take your turn. Me, I ain't in no hurry. My wife at home is just waitin' to get at me."

It didn't take much prying to learn that Mac also had an English wife. "I got me a kid, too. Just too bad it had to be a goddamned Limey." After what he apparently considered a proper tirade against the British, he filled us in on current events.

Whatever the truth of his marital affairs, he seemed to know the military situation. It didn't take long to realize that everyone was "Lieutenant Mac" to Mac. We were never to be around long enough to learn his real name. He lamented the last crew who had occupied the hut.

"He sat right where you're sittin' Lieutenant Mac. Only had two more missions to go. They didn't count any chutes."

We were to become accustomed to Private Mac's straightforwardness. Maybe his pugilistic training, mentioned in passing and obvious in appearance, taught him to hit straight from the shoulders. Each night he disappeared only to return with all the news, and always on time. Frequently he would bring a hatful of fresh eggs from what was probably the only source within miles of the base. We never questioned his methods or his motives. The eggs, fried over the potbelly at odd hours, beat anything from the cans in the mess hall. Further, there was always fuel to keep the stove cherry red most of the time and hold back the heavy dampness.

Already we had become somewhat accustomed to this dampness that shrouded the English countryside much of the time. At a placement center where we had awaited our assignment to the 44th, there was time to get the feel of both the weather and the countryside. Green fields and fence rows much like Pennsylvania made it an easy transition for me. And I enjoyed the quiet villages with their pubs and churches that vied for the restive part of men's souls.

We thought that our final assignment would bring the action for which we had waited and trained over what had been nearly a year and a half for the officers. But in terms of waiting, we were a long way from combat. Already we had been in England for nearly three weeks with nothing more exciting than a link trainer flight to liven things up.

My only form of entertainment had been censoring mail. Little things like, "I miss your warm belly against my cold back at night," as some GI pined for his wife. Or maybe it would be a grimacing form of humor such as, "I received your picture; it is very good. Ha, ha."

Rounds of classes, more link trainer followed by practice flights and test flights gave my co-pilot, Jack Emerson, a chance to find out what the '24 was all about. Jack was the boy who had joined the crew only days before we left Casper, Wyoming, to pick up our new airplane in Topeka. He didn't get much dual time at Topeka. Swinging the compass was our only flying chore before heading for Florida and points east. It took my experience to hold headings while the navigator checked his directions to eliminate as much error as possible. So, during the practice sessions over England, I let Jack handle the plane as much as possible.

It gave me a chance to think back to the emergency leave I had risked while we ground our teeth in Topeka. Thinking back took my thoughts to the new picture on the chest of drawers and to February 11. A telegram had come from my mother-in-law. "Eloise went into the hospital today." The next morning came the second telegram. "You're the father of a boy."

At 9 A.M., I was at headquarters. "My wife went to the hospital yesterday. Today I'm a father," I told the CO.

I didn't have the nerve to ask for a leave. We were on alert for overseas. In fact, officialdom held it over our heads that any infraction of the rules to stay close to quarters would result in losing our airplanes, and we would be shipped by boat. Nothing could be more degrading at this point. I might have been tempted to sneak away, but there were nine men depending on me. Consequently, I stood nervously in front of the CO, my situation in his lap. He looked at me steadily for several long moments. Finally, he glanced at his wrist watch.

"Lieutenant, it is now nine o'clock. Your leave begins at one o'clock this afternoon. Be back in thirty-six hours." I had a round trip of 2,600 miles to go.

It was my first inkling that the Army Air Force had a heart. I ran to the Red Cross building, for I didn't have the money for a train ticket. After a wasted fifteen minutes, I finally convinced the RC official that I didn't have time to get twelve signatures to prove that I was: (1) alive; (2) broke; (3) an officer and a gentleman. He assured me that this was roughly the minimum requirement to borrow $100 for three days. Finally, I changed the rules.

"Look, suppose I make out a check for the money. I

have it in my savings account at home, but my check won't be good until I get there. Just wait until I get back and *I'll* cash it.''

He mulled this over in his mind while muttering objections. I kept checking my watch, watching the precious minutes disappear. At last, and quite reluctantly, he accepted my bum check and handed me the money.

"Whatever you do, don't cash that check," was the last thing I said as I rushed from the building. Apparently he deposited it before I hit the gate.

There was a train leaving for Chicago at one o'clock. I was on it with a so-called, second class priority. Ostensibly, this meant I would be able to get a train east out of Chicago. But the ticket agent actually laughed at me when I presented it at the window. There were only minutes to spare.

"Look, Lieutenant, everybody has priorities. There's just no seat available."

I found my gate and squeezed through with the crowd. Whether the weary gateman noticed or not, he didn't even call after me. Running down along the many coaches, I jumped up the first set of empty steps and worked my way forward. When the train finally began to move, it was certain to take me closer home. How close, I wouldn't know until the conductor found me. It was surprisingly easy. He accepted my proffer of money and handed me a ticket for Harrisburg, Pennsylvania.

It was a long night, with snatches of sleep in a seat, when a seat was available. At Harrisburg, I headed for the nearest highway. In the time it would take to find a bus, if one was available, I could be on my way. And, I was on my way. I rode my thumb. It was nine o'clock, thirty-two hours from Topeka, when I ran up the steps of Geisinger Hospital in Danville.

She didn't know I was coming. But, waiting for me was the girl who dared to marry me six months ahead of schedule two years before, so that we could have a few months before I enlisted. It was the same girl who had followed me from base to base around the country. A cadet wife, married to the lowest rank in the service. But now she was an officer's wife and a very sick one—though I did not know it then.

It was the last tenderness I was to know for a long time to come. We broke every rule in the hospital, the one where she learned to become a nurse, wife, and mother. And finally, one of the nurses sneaked a bundle from the nursery. She informed me that the tiny creature inside the blanket was our son.

Babies had always looked about alike to me. This one didn't look much different. Gazing at that fragile, new person, I suddenly felt that the war was much less grim. Here was a part of me that would continue on regardless of what happened. He even had my name over my protests. I was suddenly glad, glad that everything was exactly as it was. I ran down the hospital steps with tears of happiness streaming down my face. Even then, the incongruity of it all insisted that I was a fool. I was running away from everything I had wanted out of life to that point, but I was supremely happy, and so proud.

Berwick is only twenty-two miles from Danville. The folks at home explained that Eloise was dangerously ill. My leave was already too far gone. The next morning I talked to the doctors. The head obstetrician was gentle with me, too gentle.

"There is something we can't define at this point," he explained. "But I think Eloise will be all right."

I suspected more than they were telling me. After explaining my situation, I asked, "Do you think I should still ask for an extension of my leave?" The answer was affirmative.

Topeka said no. Get back at once. I rushed to the bank to pick up money to cover my bad check and made air reservations to prolong my visit as much as possible. But bad weather again forced me to take the train, and I was a day late getting back. Fortunately, nothing was said. Then we sat around Topeka for another fourteen days before heading overseas. It was time enough to learn that my wife would recover. It was also time enough to discover that I would have to wire back the money to cover my still bad check.

And now, in England, we were playing the old army game again. Each day we would rush to the bulletin board to see if we were scheduled for combat. Jack was ready. So was Dale Raushcher, my navigator, and Larry Davis, the bombardier.

Just as ready was the rest of the crew: Engineer Bill Sanders who would also handle the twin 50's in the top turret; his assistant, George Renfro, with the added duty of manning the left waist gun; Harry Schow, with his own pair of 50's in the tail turret; George Cox, at the flexible gun at the other waist window; Walt Reichert, who was small enough to fit well into the retractable ball turret under the plane's belly; and Leonard Rowland, the quiet one who did most of his talking on his radios. All were sergeants and each represented some different part of the United States.

We were not much different from the average crew of a B-24 bomber. Each had his own reason for being there. In the main, we had the average desire to serve our country in a time of obvious need. We sought the glamour of the flying war, the excitement. Maybe we had a little more than average crew esprit de corps; maybe we were a little more eager than the average. But, for all crews there could be no doubt of the need to do a job.

Aside from those reasons, which I shared, I had three personal purposes. First, I thought that flying offered an *easy* way to a commission. I was wrong. Secondly, I wanted to come back in one piece or not at all. I thought the Air Force provided the way until I saw what a 20 mm, burning gasoline, a chunk of flak, or a sprinkling of 30-caliber bullets could leave alive of a kid who flew. Finally, I was married and wanted a job that would support a wife while I was in service. This it did.

But now, as March slid into April, all the previous training, the pent-up energy and the desire to test our fighting skills made each hour drag. We had developed a healthy respect for the vagaries of the weather, and a little fear, but we were combat-ready. So we thought.

It was the weather that held us up as much as anything. Too thick to breathe and too thin to drink, fogs wrapped the base in a milky package that even the Germans didn't often try to penetrate in the daytime. Night was different.

As the infrequent sun splashed down somewhere beyond the mist, the British would roar out to battle. Singly, they rumbled out over the tops of ground clouds to admit the gaze of curious stars. We shuddered for them, wondering where they found the courage to take on the enemy in the black of night. And, we were told that they shuddered for the fool Yanks. Crazy Americans, who took over in the mornings to crawl across fields of flak with their bellies exposed to hot steel from below while painting stark targets against the blue canvas for the Luftwaffe.

Somehow, this morbid sympathy for the seeming stupidity of others drew us to these magnificent Britishers. They had held the line somewhere out over the water before the Americans came. But all of their warm blood so freely spilled had failed to raise the frigid temperature of the clutching North Sea that was both their defense and their enemy.

It was one such star-studded night that we had our first feel of the war.

"Red alert; this is a red alert!" the loudspeaker insisted, and we quickly blacked out our hut. We had done this frequently before, but nothing ever came of it. Now Jerry was in the immediate area. The four of us stepped out into the chill. Stalks of searchlights waved across the heavens and the drone of hidden airplanes took on a new meaning.

Then one of the probing lights found a target! Immediately, two more lights converged on the spot. Clearly outlined was the gray cross of an airplane. Instinctively, we braced for the crash of guns. But beneath the belly of the plane a light blinked. The searchlights went out. The signal of the British pilot had been unmistakable. We all shared his sigh of relief.

Again the searchlights shot aloft. But the action drifted south where the guns now went into action, a distant *krump, krump,* and flashes like heat lightning, impersonal. We began to notice the chill for the first time. Our war had again evaded us.

But not for long.

3

The clouds have opened once again for them
To clear a stormless trail that leads beyond the sun
Unto the shelter of a Peaceful Nest
Where tired birdmen settle when their work is done.

And we who linger here on borrowed time,
Within the deepened shadow of life's overcast,
But pray that we may rise to fly again
Until the tower clears us for that flight at last.

From "For Them"

"Schuyler, Schuyler."

The words were soft in my semiconsciousness, yet insistent, a whispered command.

"Are you awake?"

The solitary bulb by the doorway to the Nissen hut came at me like a sheet of light, then subsided into its proper perspective. For the first time, I realized that the squadron CO was sitting on the edge of my cot, a half silhouette in the dim light of the bulb and my still foggy vision.

I mumbled out a "Yeah, I'm awake."

"Look. I'm sorry to wake you up like this. But"—the CO was being apologetic—"we're leading the 8th Air Force this morning, and the group is putting on a maximum effort. Do you think you could make the mission?"

21

It was like asking me if I thought I could breathe. Even as I bolted upright and the CO moved away so that I could roll out, my mind came fully alive. A hundred questions crowded in upon my carefully planned reply.

"Sure we can make it."

But why? Why had he suddenly dragged me out in the middle of the night when we weren't even considered combat-ready as a crew? I had been sweating out the bulletin board for my first ride across the North Sea with an experienced pilot before taking my crew. It was usual for replacement pilots to tackle their first mission as copilot with an experienced crew.

The second crew, with a pilot I'll call Stenson, was also stirring for this one. But Stenson had ridden once with Lieutenant Winchester, the same fellow it was rumored I was to fly with on my first. Not over three hours before, the eight of us had been shooting craps around the iron monster and sipping coffee and hot chocolate while bemoaning our inactivity. The last thing I had remembered before the CO awakened me was Stenson's bombardier feeding me chocolate from a spoon as I lay under the blankets.

Leading the 8th Air Force! It sounded like a real honor. And I guess in a way it was. They say there is honor in dying for your country.

A big section of the group that gathered in the briefing room were to be so honored that day. Grim faces on the experienced crews around us provided the first clue as the room gradually filled with smoke and bulky bodies covered by sheepskin-lined leather. Yellow Mae West life preservers over the leather provided the only contrast other than faces pale with strain and lack of sleep.

The moderate hubbub subsided quickly as the briefing officer stepped to the platform and reached for the catch on the map case. He unreeled it downward with a quick sweep of his arm. The flap of the map was drowned by an audible moan that swept the room.

"Yes, it's going to be a rough one." His pointer easily found the superimposed marks on the map. "We'll be hitting a target near Hanover, here,'' his pointer indicated. ''You know what that means.'' I didn't. ''We expect heavy flak over the target area, and you can expect to be hit by fighters. There are still plenty of them left.'' He traced our route and procedures. So many times before we had gone through this routine. Now it had a new, grim meaning. Then the room darkened and aerial photos were projected of the target area.

We broke up so that the navigators and bombardiers could have separate briefings. The squadron CO explained assignments so that each man would know where he was to fly. Most of the older pilots knew their positions, but there were a few minor changes to make. I hadn't been mentioned. Another replacement, a Lieutenant Sprinkle, and I were all who were left. Finally, the captain turned to me.

''Schuyler, we don't have a place for you and Sprinkle. So you just tag along until you find a place to fill in. We're putting up everything that will fly, and we expect to have some abortions. As soon as somebody pulls out, you take their place wherever it is.''

I was green, but not too green to realize that I would be flying the coffin corner . . . outside edge of the rear where flak was more likely to find you. It was bad enough sitting in the back row, the position reserved for newcomers but not to have even an assigned position left me with a worthless and empty feeling. As though reading my thoughts, the captain tried to console me. ''Don't worry, Schuyler. You will probably find a place to move in.''

He turned to Sprinkle. ''Sprinkle, as soon as Schuyler finds a place, you take the next opening.'' At least I wasn't last man.

Sprinkle looked at me and grinned. ''If somebody pulls out, I'll give you just two minutes to take his place or I'm filling in.'' He was smiling, but I knew he meant it.

I couldn't help stealing an occasional look at Stenson. He still had the same cocksure attitude that had made him unpopular with the other replacements from the day he arrived. He had his first ride as co-pilot behind him, and this increased his cockiness. I sympathized with his other officers who had confided to me that they could hardly bear his attitude. There was constant bickering among them. And my enlisted men had reported the same lack of confidence among Stenson's enlisted men. Of course, this was his twentieth birthday, and he had every right to take pride in the fact that he was probably the youngest airplane commander on the base.

It wasn't that Stenson wasn't a good pilot. He was. But my thoughts drifted back to the night Captain Sakowski dropped into our Nissen hut. He was from Wilkes-Barre, Pennsylvania, and he had heard that I was from Berwick, only thirty miles away. Sakowski was lead navigator for the group. He shared our coffee while joshing us about our impatience to get going.

"Don't worry, fellows, you'll see plenty of action. New crews are badly needed. But we're short on airplanes, too." We plied him with questions about actual combat. "It can be rough," he emphasized. "But some days you have a real milk run when you expect real trouble. Other times, it looks like a snap and you get the hell kicked out of you."

What about fighters?

"They can be tough. They pick out one group and plaster it. If you happen to be the group, you get hurt. Otherwise, you might see plenty of them and never get touched."

Stenson kept interrupting. Each time Sakowski answered a question, we would also get Stenson's version of the answer.

What about flak?

"Well, it can be worse than fighters. The minute you see it, have the boys in the back start throwing out chaff. That metal tinsel really goofs up the tracking mechanism for the gun crews on the ground. Usually it is roughest at the tail end of the formation because the gunners track on the lead planes. If they miss the main part of the formation, they can still pick off stragglers. Hold it in close."

"Do you ever get flak and fighters at the same time?" Everybody was asking questions, particularly me.

"Not usually. The Krauts don't like to fly into their own flak. But if they're around, they move in as soon as the flak lets up." And this I was never to forget: "If the fighters come in on you, move. I don't care which way you move, up or down or sidewise, but move. They have to aim their airplanes, and you can throw them off. You might still get hit, but they won't hit you where they expect to."

Now, in the briefing room, Sakowski was with the other navigators getting final instructions. We had been sweating out each mission for him as he neared the end of his tour. If he got through this one, he would have his twenty-five and a pass to the States. What a mission to finish up on!

The squadron CO didn't pull his punches. "You might as well know it. The Krauts often gang up on the lead group, hoping to foul up the groups behind."

What he didn't tell us, but we had heard, was that the fighters often concentrated on the lead airplane itself. They had learned that the group of airplanes behind would drop their bombs on the leader's signal. The signal was simply the release, the sudden appearance of bombs dropping. In saturation bombing, it wasn't necessary to have a bomb sight on every plane. This was a source of real disgust for the well-trained bombardiers who bristled at the title of "toggleier."

As we climbed onto the trucks for a trip to the dispersal area, it was so different physically from many trips we had made before. Our eagerness was only slightly subdued by the serious attitude of seasoned crews who were silent or in quiet communication with their fellows.

It was a new experience to climb up past the gray blobs of metal hanging ominously in their racks as we swung into the bomb bay and moved to the flight deck after a visual check of the aircraft. I felt a sense of power and a great weight of responsibility as I slid into the left seat and adjusted my safety belt. Chatter of the men over the interphone soon brought me to the realization that this would be just another flight mechanically, whatever the implications.

We were ready some time before the flare to "start engines" broke the fading darkness. I nudged number three, the right inboard engine, into life and took a certain satisfaction in this first real move toward the start of our first mission. Then its mate on the outside roared in, then number two, number one. Finally all four Pratts were tugging against the brakes while the crew chief stood nervously by observing the effects of his handiwork. We had been told back in the States by returning fliers that this was the one man upon whom you put the most reliance in combat. As we sat waiting our turn to taxi, I felt the first real sense of kinship with this man upon whom our very lives might depend in the part of this day for which he had prepared. I didn't even remember the name he gave me when we met before climbing aboard, but I knew he would be flying with us for every turn of those props until we returned. If we returned. . . .

It was an even longer wait before I could taxi out behind the tail lights that marked the bomber ahead of me. And, it seemed forever before we were finally lined up on the runway. Only Sprinkle waited for our takeoff. Then we started rolling, at first a mere crawl as the 4800 horses screamed into the morning air.

The ship had a heavy feel with a full load of gasoline and the rows of bombs in her belly, but she finally lightened and lifted from the concrete as I pointed her after the tail lights ahead. At 3,000 feet and still groaning upward, I was ready for a smoke. Jack took over.

I needed that smoke. For, already I suspected that I was in for trouble. The right wing seemed heavy. As soon as I dropped back the propeller pitch after getting airborne, the heaviness in the wing became more obvious. By the time Jack took over, I had applied all the trim available to keep her level.

Our assembly altitude was 15,000 feet. At 12,000 feet the number four supercharger went out. The other three engines took a mighty pounding getting us up that last

3,000 feet. Already my gasoline was getting too low for the time aloft.

It was no trouble finding an opening. Several airplanes failed to make it even to this altitude. Our group was flying in three boxes, and I headed for an opening in the first. We couldn't make it. Finally, I was able to tag on to the third section. And, as we swung into formation on the right wing of the last element, a new problem developed.

With the right wing dragging, it was impossible to hold formation. We kept swinging back and forth out of position. It seemed that each time we slid out, and I lifted the right wing to get back in, we would slide dangerously close to the man on our left. I was working as hard as that first day in Tennessee when I labored to learn to land a B-24.

We crossed the coast of Holland and headed inland. On our left, a group flew safely through a barrage of flak, the first we had seen. It needed no identification: filthy black stuff that drifted back through the formation with no apparent effect, but ominous in its implication. As we crossed the Zuider Zee, I was caught between the desire to make this mission and to save the plane and crew. With only 1,500 gallons of gasoline showing on the indicators of the 2,700 we had loaded, we had no margin of safety. With fifteen miles remaining to cross the German border, my mind was made up for me.

Several times it had been necessary to pull up and drop back to avoid hitting the man on my left. Each time it took precious fuel to work my way back into formation. Then, on one swing back, I could no longer control the bomber. It was as though a giant wind suddenly swept me toward the formation. I pulled the nose and jammed all four throttles full forward. We barely missed the nearest bomber and swung out over the formation with the plane shuddering like a sick cat from the supreme effort of the engines.

I couldn't fly with the formation. It was suicide to fly as satellite and give up protection afforded by the other bombers. Anyway, there already was a serious question as to whether we could make the full mission on our dwindling gasoline supply.

We swung away and I headed on Rauscher's vector for home.

It was a humiliating experience for all of us. We had strained at the leash for over a month waiting for this day. And now we were headed the wrong direction with a load of bombs that we had been trained to drop on the enemy. Overhead, hundreds of friendly fighters winged toward Germany. We didn't ask for cover. That would have been the crowning humiliation. However, at the Dutch coast, a P-51 fighter picked us up and escorted us all the way back to the English coast.

On the way I had a chance to experiment with the controls without the hazard of ramming another airplane. I found that the wing would lift about 20 degrees without much difficulty. But then, it would whip up and throw us to the left almost out of control. It seemed as though the full trim necessary to hold level flight would suddenly grab air and throw the big wing another 20 degrees or so.

As we neared the coast, Davis asked me to circle to pick a spot to unload our bombs. With the plane misbehaving, a landing with the twelve 500-pound bombs could be disastrous to us as well as the base. We jettisoned the entire load.

After an uneventful landing, I headed for engineering. They assured me that the airplane had flown okay in test flight, but it was flown without a load. They did admit that a Ford wing had been attached to a Consolidated fuselage after the bomber had been wrecked. This really shouldn't have made any difference. Possibly it was a combination of a dead supercharger on the outside engine of that wing, plus the full trim needed to overcome an aerodynamic deficiency, that caused the trouble. We never found out. The airplane was not put back into service during our brief stay.

Other than engineering, the department that ever seemed ready to uphold its opinions regardless of a pilot's report, there was no hint of criticism over our abortion. Four other bombers, sore and stiff from countless missions, had failed to make it. Like an old dog that responds to the smells and sound of the first day of hunting season, each hobbled out and up, only to return to the kennel shame-faced as the crews that couldn't complete their trip.

But there were still thirty-nine of our group out there somewhere, leading the 8th to something that we could only surmise. It had taken us four hours and thirty-five minutes to get to the fringe of Germany and back. Only the gray sky of afternoon held the answers for the others.

Then reports began to filter through.

The 44th had had the living hell knocked out of it! Losses were heavy. We didn't know how heavy until the battered bombers began to limp back to base. Some had to land elsewhere as dwindling fuel and battle damage forced them to seek the nearest refuge. Three ships ground-looped on landing with flat tires shot empty of air by flak, machine guns or 20-mm cannon. Finally, the results were in.

Eleven of the thirty-nine bombers had been shot down!

Near the target, the fighters caught them. Attacking with more than usual savagery, they smashed through the for-mations pouring a hail of fire into the lumbering '24's.

Those near Stenson told how he had bought it. It seemed likely that his ship had caught a bad burst right in the pilot's compartment. The big airplane had simply turned over and went straight down with all four engines churn-ing. Sprinkle, the boy who had taken my place when I pulled away, was the second victim. A damaged enemy fighter had smashed into Winn, a boy I had flown with since transition back in Tennessee. Both went down to-gether.

Out of the ten replacement crews who had made up the contingent of which our crew was a part, five went down that day before Easter, April 8, 1944. But Sakowski, and we thanked God for him, had made it back in a ship full of holes. His tour was finished. It was also finished for 110 men in the eleven bombers that had vanished somewhere over Germany. There were many empty chairs in the mess hall that evening.

The hardest part was returning to our Nissen hut. Stenson's wife still smiled down toward his cot, and odds and ends of personal effects of the crew stood neglected on the tables and hung along the walls. Again the hut seemed large and cold. There was a half-empty K ration box sitting by the stove.

We had felt our war.

My name was up for the Easter parade.

4

I've found the hidden rainbows that you hold
  With which to tie your ribboned gifts of rain;
Gifts much more precious than the pots of gold;
  For gold can never rise to bless again.

I've sought your secrets in the darkest path,
  Where but the fearsome lightning dares to tread,
And felt the wild fury of your wrath
  Within the bitter bowels of thunderhead.
                    From "Oh Clouds; My Clouds"

Fighting the weather over England was the most frustrating battle of the air war. It was one thing to risk the wrath of enemy planes and ground fire to get your bombs on target. It was only natural that the Germans would fight back. But fighting the clammy mists and rolling clouds that covered the British Isles at the whim of the weather was yet another.

Meteorologists were even more frustrated than we. For we had only to follow orders. It was their reports upon which were based the orders to fly or to stand down. If the weathermen guessed wrong, the results could be costly. Many men could die needlessly without ever approaching the German battlements. For much of England was dotted with air fields. Each had to have an air pattern of trails for the heavies to climb on their way over the North Sea or the English Channel. It was tough enough in the light of day getting hundreds of bombers off the ground and assembled in the air for the trip east. When the weather socked in suddenly, the result was chaos.

Such a day was Easter, April 9, 1944.

Our target was the Kiel Canal. The moans when the briefing officer's pointer found it for us were somewhat subdued. At least we would be flying over water most of the way up and back. Although we were told that a man could survive only twenty minutes in the frigid waters of the North Sea, we preferred this risk to braving the guns of the Luftwaffe and the flak batteries over land.

"Flak will be heavy over Kiel," the officer warned as he pointed out the city at the northeast end of the 61-mile canal. "And there are a number of fighter bases on the Friesian Islands which guard the entrance to the Elbe River."

It was not difficult to understand why the Allies wanted the canal knocked out. It was the only direct waterway between the North Sea and the Baltic. One of the most important ship canals of the world, its locks provided available length greater than the mighty Panama Canal. It was important to the Germans, and it was defended accordingly.

However, our concern was not with logistics of the canal or the important harbor at Kiel. It was the weather report that worried us most.

"There is a front moving in," the weather officer said, "but we think you can get out ahead of it." He didn't say how we would get back.

A part of the front was already rolling in as we began to gain altitude after takeoff. We found ourselves boxed in an area several miles across by clouds on all sides. However, vertical clearance was good, and we could still see the ground. Our group decided to assemble on the way up in the big hole.

We were not the only planes taking advantage of the open space. On the other side, directly across from us as we made a too-tight circle while attempting to build our formation, was another group of B-24's. I found myself stealing glimpses at the military procession of bombers straining to meet a destiny outlined for them only a short time before in another briefing room.

All at once, the dim sky split apart in the monumental crash of a giant fire ball.

For a hellish instant, this sudden sun of red-black flame splashed its hue against every airplane and the walls of mist for miles around. Then it died, in a slow moment that saw defiant tongues of flame succumb to a filthy black sphere of smoke that replaced the explosion. The sphere hovered in place, a dirty, dark monument to twenty men and two great bombers now shredded to bits.

Below the ball, some of the bits dropped swiftly as tiny blobs of debris. A few larger ones, still flaming, undulated downward, their descent marked by a twisting spiral of thin black smoke. Somehow, unbelievably, out of the debris blossomed five parachutes. We could only morbidly surmise what the harnesses below the white umbrellas now held. Over 5,000 gallons of high test gasoline and 10,400 pounds of incendiary bombs had been in those two airplanes.

Within seconds, flame from the ground indicated that not all the incendiaries had exploded aloft. The collision had occurred over an air base. One end of a hangar was burning fiercely. There were other fires, too.

But our job was not to watch fires, or to give more than a passing prayer for the unknown airmen who had found their way to die far from enemy skies. We had a mission to fly. Anyway, we were above the ball of smoke when we circled the other side of the hole.

A heavy haze developed shortly after we left the English coast to warn that warm air of the expected front had preceded us. Vapor trails began to pour from the slipstream of each plane as propellers agitated the touchy atmosphere and turned moisture-laden air into artificial clouds. As we traveled through each layer of critical air, vapor trails marked advancement of the front. Then, as we lifted to the higher air, where the lower temperatures squeezed moisture out of the warm front climbing over the cool air that preceded it, clouds blocked our way.

At first they were thin, and it was no great task to hold position. But then we were engulfed in solid sheets of clouds several hundred feet in thickness. We emerged from one layer with the bomber that had been on our left now on our right! Planes were turning back, passing those still forging ahead within the black bowels of the gray barriers. I shuddered inwardly, memories of less than an hour sickeningly fresh in my mind.

Somewhere in the churning mists we lost our element, and I tagged onto the first available bomber. When that one turned back, I found another. Finally, that one peeled away and headed back to England. As I broke out of the clouds, at last ahead of the advancing front, I saw a formation of nine airplanes grouped below me. I held altitude until they reached my level, then I swung into formation with them. Although mixed markings represented several groups, most of the squadron was from one outfit. But at least we were on our way to *some* target, and we had 5,200 pounds of incendiary bombs for whatever target had been assigned.

We had passed the West Friesians, dim off the right wing, and were almost in sight of Germany when the formation suddenly turned and headed back to England. There were no other ships in sight. We had no choice but to turn with the nine. Even as we were turning, Jack switched to interphone.

"Just got a recall from the squadron lead," he announced.

Somewhere at least a part of our group was together, and they were heading home. I called to Rauscher for a heading back to base. We were now approaching the main part of the front which topped at 20,000 feet with a brilliant expanse of wooly backs as far as the eye could see. In moments the navigator gave me my heading and I swung away from the formation on course. Skimming tops of the sunlit cloud cover, I felt relatively safe from fighters if any were so foolish as to brave this weather to find us. Under the sun, the clouds which had so unnerved us a few hours before now provided a friendly invitation to safety if we needed them. Jack switched back to interphone and gave me a heading.

I nodded. "I know." And I pointed to the compass.

"What do you mean, you know?" He looked at me curiously. "I just received the heading from our base."

I pointed at the compass again. The heading he had just received was exactly the same as Rauscher had given me for home! I mentally marked down an A-plus for our fine little navigator.

As we neared England it was necessary once more to dip into the uncertainty of the stormy maelstrom that looked so soft and innocent from above. Although there were pockets of clear air at various altitudes, it made little difference in the gray darkness of these misty spaces. I kept thinking of the incendiaries we still carried, and I needed no urging from Davis to seek an opening to dispose of our load. At 2,000 feet we found a clearing that revealed a dark expanse of water. After several circles to ensure that the area was clear, Larry jettisoned the load.

As the bombs hit almost simultaneously, they formed a pattern like a huge burning ship on the surface.

We grabbed a little more altitude and tried to raise the base of the 44th. Our radio proved to be inoperative. I finally picked up home on the VHF set. We were told that the base was socked in almost to the runway. Dropping down, I strained for a glimpse of the marker lights and finally found a trace of them through the mist.

Our first pass was too far down the runway. I circled at low altitude, trying to keep visual contact, and lined up for another pass. Again, we saw only enough reference points to keep us in a relative position with the field. Our second pass was too far off to attempt a safe landing. Then word came from the field that a new type of flare was being lit, and they asked that we make special mental note on its effectiveness. If this didn't work, the tower informed me, the landing beam would be turned on. We could ride it in by sound. I would have welcomed the chance to utilize my link trainer experience under normal circumstances, but this was for real. I preferred a visual landing if possible.

Although the flares were bright enough, when we could see them, they could not cut the haze. Nevertheless, I could see enough at brief intervals to finally make a proper approach. We slid on in without further difficulty.

Fifteen minutes after we touched the ground, the sun was shining brightly.

We had spent six hours and forty-five minutes in the air, two of which were recorded as instrument time. But this was not a mission. The only enemy encountered was the weather. This would be a bit difficult to accept for the crews that had gone down in the collision or for the two pilots of our group who ran off the runway because of the weather on their landings.

Seven of our airplanes had hit the target with another group to which they had attached when unable to assemble with the scattered 44th. One of the seven had to land in Sweden, but the other six came home safely.

5

Our hearts roared, raging, throbbing louder then
Above the eager engines' blatant beat.
While the bow-string nerves of a thousand men
Sent quick commands to frigid hands and feet.
From "First Time to the Target"

We had wanted to fight. Now it became evident that we were to get a bellyful, and fast. Only the weather held us down on the tenth, but on April 11, we were again up early for our third trip in four days.

This time we felt some of the apprehension that swept the group when the map was lowered and the pointer directed our attention deep into Germany. Our job was to knock out an airport near Bernberg, one of those in a spray of bases that fanned out to protect Berlin. It would be a long hop for the '24's, nearly six hundred miles one way as the crow flies. Because of the distance our load was light, 240 little fragmentation bombs that weighed only twenty-three pounds a piece—less than three tons.

It was not the load this time. But the target was in "one of the hottest flak and fighter areas of Europe. Get in and get out," the briefing officer said, more by word of warning than by order. "Be ready to expect heavy flak all through the area. We have tried to give you a course that will avoid most of it, but we can never be sure that they haven't moved more guns in. You're hitting an air field; tell your gunners to keep their eyes open." He didn't have to tell us that the Luftwaffe would be out to protect its nest. But it was some consolation to learn that three Royal Air Force groups flying American P-51 fighters were supposed to rendezvous with us over the target area.

As we listened to instructions, I for the first time began to feel a part of this group of grim-faced men who had been boys only a matter of days or weeks or months ago. I didn't feel quite so much a mere appendage to a war machine that moved on mysterious orders relayed at these briefings and operated on gasoline and guts. Some of the faces were becoming more familiar, and an occasional nod gave an impression that my presence was of some importance to others than my squadron CO. I had been voted in, but the members were maintaining a cautious reserve until I passed the initiation.

"You'll be flying left wing on the first element of the low box," I was told as the formation was outlined.

This would move us forward from the tail end of the group. Ahead and several hundred feet higher would be the lead box. Pacing us, but at an equally higher elevation on our right would be the high box. This arrangement assured a tight bombing pattern when viewed from above or below, but it gave each box its own air to cut into without bouncing in the propwash of the other bombers.

Our assigned airplane, the *Wasp Nest*,* was another of the battered hulks that somehow flew. Sergeant Cox was grounded by a case of hives, and a Sergeant Rachor was in his place at the right waist gun. Everything else seemed normal as we lined up on the runway for takeoff. This time we were ahead of nine or ten other bombers waiting their turn on the taxi strip. I stood on the brakes and moved the throttles forward until the manifold pressure gauges

---

* The *Wasp Nest* went down in July, 1944, in a collision with a plane of the 506th Squadron on the way to Bremen, Germany. William Green was the pilot, and all aboard were lost. (From the book, *History of the 68th Squadron, 44th Bomb Group*.)

showed thirty inches. Then I turned her loose. Our bomb load was light, and we should have plenty of runway.

"Close bomb doors," I called, and we rolled. Manifold pressure responded to a normal forty-nine inches.

But, this morning something was wrong. The plane felt sluggish. The nose came up slowly. And our roll didn't seem to be picking up with the normal zest. As the air speed needles approached 120 mph, I felt for lift and there was no response. Quickly I snapped the wheel back to level to streamline the elevators, grabbing for every fraction of speed. We were beyond the point of cutting out. I had to try for takeoff! I hit the emergency button on the manifold pressure and grabbed a dangerous fifty-five inches.

Now I concentrated visually on the runway, taking all I dared. Finally, the end of the concrete rushed at us, forcing my hand. Stealing a quick glance at the air speed, 120, I eased back on the wheel. I felt her lift—ponderously, tiredly. "Gear up!" We just cleared a fence, and I held her down for a precious few seconds, making a quick check of an opening through the trees ahead. Not enough space for a whole airplane. Then we hit the hole, and I raised the left wing to clear the top branches. It lifted shudderingly, the bomber on the fringe of a stall and destruction. Beyond, fields. I eased her down, taking advantage of even thirty or forty feet to gain speed.

As the fence rows snapped beneath us, I began to feel strength returning to the airplane. The sloppy controls firmed; we were flying. I pointed our nose upward and felt sweat inside the rabbit-lined gloves Eloise had sent me.

We were well above the shrinking fields before I eased off the manifold pressure. At 3,000 feet, I dared to look at Jack and Sergeant Bill Sanders. Only they could know how close we had come to finishing our tour in an English cow pasture. Neither had moved a muscle from the time Sanders had hit the lever to raise the landing gear to "flaps up." Their faces were white in the faint glow of morning.

"Take her, Jack," I said, and lit a cigarette. We exchanged sickly grins.

We always took advantage of the air space between 3,000 and 10,000 to light up before going on oxygen. Near ground level, it was too dangerous to light a match. Always, we taxied and ran up the engines against the brakes for takeoff with the bomb doors open. To get every mile of flight out of the engines, it was necessary to top the tanks with gasoline which often slopped over and ran down inside the bomb bay to create dangerous fumes. It had been learned the hard way that any spark could ignite these fumes.

Most men can operate with efficiency under normal activity up to 12,000 feet. However, I ordered oxygen on at 10,000. There was no way of knowing when we might be called on for a maximum effort at any altitude.

I could steal occasional glances at Jack Emerson when he was at work. And I liked what I saw. Even as we headed for enemy territory with him at the controls, I was cognizant of the fact that this young man from Santa Monica, California, had been roughly thrust into a responsibility that was not to his liking. Yet, he was uncomplaining. A head taller than I, his easygoing disposition paced my rather methodical approach to things; and he was steady.

In fact, his overcasual approach had California written all over it. But, reckless, blondish hair topping a freckle-sprinkled light complexion made Jack a boyish candidate for any college campus in the states. Mild blue eyes, with a hint of fire, belied a physical and mental reserve that had to be called upon but were ever ready. He would still blush admirably when kidded about Phoebe, the girl on the return address of most of his mail. We had talked seriously about his immediate future when en route to England.

"Jack, I know it must have been a letdown to be sent out as co-pilot on a bomber. But one thing I promise you— the moment I think you are ready for your own crew, I'll recommend you."

This was not an idle promise. I felt for these kids who

thought they had it made as first pilot even as I did when fighter training was snatched away from me. But the prospects of losing a second co-pilot after training him was not to my liking. There seemed to be no permanency in anything related to being a replacement. I was riding into war with a young man I hardly knew and our lives were in each other's hands.

This morning we assembled as we climbed toward the rising sun. At 13,000 feet, our group was together when we approached the Dutch coast. Ahead of us was another group headed for the same target, and it began to get flak—heavy flak. Flanking us were other groups, and we came up on the coast together at various altitudes. Then we were in the flak.

The barrage was heavy, and it was close. For the first time we were in close proximity to the death being exploded at us. Like thunder, the black marking charges burst around and under our airplanes while the unseen lightning groped for metal and flesh. For the first time we could hear the pop of the close ones. We were riding it well, but off to the left another group was not so favored. Davis called it.

"A B-24 is on fire off our left wing," he said, not completely able to hide the excitement of his report. Only moments later, "There goes another!"

Rauscher's eyes had been grinning back at me from the astrodome in the center of the forward fuselage when the action started. But now he had ducked back to his charts. I took Davis's word for the crippled planes. "Watch for chutes," I answered. Evasive action by our group was taking all my attention as I hugged the formation. Close bursts of ground fire would rock the Liberator to further complicate attempts to hold close flying order.

Then we were out of it. But, subconsciously all of us were aware that it would be there waiting on our return trip. The German border was just ahead, and this time it looked as though we would finally be over enemy territory. Rauscher's head bounced back up into the astrodome. From a fishing rod's length, his eyes again grinned back at me over his oxygen mask. Then he pointed to a spot in the dome. For the first time I could see a jagged hole in the heavy plexiglas. About the size of a little finger.

"Flak," Dale said over interphone. "It wrecked an oxygen bottle and smashed into the radar equipment." This ship was equipped with experimental radar equipment which was now inoperative.

Had the little navigator not ducked down from the dome to attend his charts, the hot metal would have smashed through his head or body rather than to bury itself in the aircraft accessories.

Now we were crossing the German border. It was a certain satisfaction to realize that at last we were in the battlefield for which we had trained so long and so hard. Our satisfaction was short-lived. Flak was coming up again.

Ahead of us the groups were taking a pounding. The scene would blossom again and again with patterns of the black puff balls, ugly mushrooms that sprouted in a now familiar form and then disintegrated in the thin air. Our group leader skirted the obvious trouble spots, profiting from troubles of preceding airplanes. But again, off to the left, flak was pasting a group of bombers.

One of them caught fire. Burning fiercely, it pulled wide of the formation and dropped fast. Two parachutes were left behind, slowly undulating downward. The bomber tore itself apart with fire and wind as it hurried to complete destruction.

As we groped our way deeper and deeper into German skies, a pair of B-24's became evident, flying unattended, each in its own part of the morning sky. They just sat out there, at our altitude, pacing the formation. Renfro called them out from the left waist window.

"I can't make out any markings on them," he said. "I wonder what they are doing out there."

"If you can't read any markings, and they get close to us, fire at them," I directed the crew. "No one in his right mind would sit out there alone—unless they are

Krauts flying them.'' We had been warned that the Germans were using captured airplanes. Flak was coming up again, at first sporadic and inaccurate. Now, as if to confirm my suspicions of the strange '24's, the ground fire zeroed in on our formation. Flak became heavy, and it was right at the level of our lead box. There were no apparent bad hits, for our formation continued on. And now, friendly fighters moved overhead, an umbrella of protection that warmed our hearts and bolstered confidence somewhat shaken by the nearby losses.

Within thirty minutes of the target, flak seemed to be everywhere. It freckled the sky at all altitudes, scatter shots that guessed at a target. As we approached the IP to turn for our target, our little friends upstairs had to head for home. They should soon be replaced by the R.A.F. fighters, according to schedule. Down below, smoke screens were covering some targets and providing good wind information as the artificial white clouds billowed across the ground.

Finally we turned for our run, and bomb-bay doors began to open. I nudged the trim tabs to compensate for added drag and swung in tight to the element leader. Flak was still in evidence, but it was no problem. Still, we had been promised at least thirty flak guns right over the target. Heavy stuff.

It came. Not only flak, but fighters!

At first, we only saw a few enemy fighters at a distance as they circled for the kill. We marked them. Flak became intense, and we didn't expect the Jerries to fly into it.

Then, out of the sun, two silver shapes flashed in toward the high box. Messerschmitt 109's they were, deadly beautiful as they rolled in through the formation, bright yellow dots marking the bursts of their cannons. Faint traces of smoke swept back in their slipstreams as their guns hammered through the formation. And, tracers from the bombers stenciled a faint red code against the perfect blue backdrop of sky. I called them out for Sanders in the top turret, but he was busy.

Two M.E.'s had cut in from the left. The engineer's twin fifties were already stuttering out a reply to this threat.

With Sakowski's advice well marked in my memory, I was kicking our bomber wildly within the confines of our sky and our formation. There wasn't much room to move. I took it all while keeping close watch on the element lead. No one was on my wing, but it was close to bombs away, and I dared not stray. Possibly a fifty-foot square box held our deviation from straight and level. It may have been good strategy.

Unknown to me, two more M.E.'s and a Focke Wulf 190 were boring in from the rear. Renfro and Rachor, Cox's substitute, were busy throwing out metallic chaff when another 190 swept by a plane's width away. Renfro dove for his gun and blasted away until it jammed. Meanwhile, Schow had fired a burst from the tail twins into the M.E.'s on our left without visible effect.

In the seconds for this all to happen, our group had come through whole. Now my guns were silent, but my interphone was alive. I could follow the action behind through the eyes of my gunners.

"There goes a '24! It must have been a direct hit. He blew all to hell! Looks like another one on fire; his engine's smoking. He's dropping out, dropping out. My God! There he goes. Blew up!"

"Hey, look at his tail section. It's all by itself." Then, "The gunner's out. There goes his chute."

Two more B-24's took the count in the groups behind us. Both flamers. My gunners painted the gory picture for me as again I slid in tight. Now there would be no more moving. It was time for bombs away. I took a quick glance at the lead squadron and the high box to see if they were still intact. They were, for the moment.

But, my eyes caught and hung for an instant on the outside element of the high box. A burst of flak marked itself just beneath a bomber. Immediately, flames started to pour from the bomb bay.

At the same instant, bombs began dropping, and I steadied our airplane. I felt her lift as the load flashed from our racks, and I heard Davis call, "Close bomb doors." My hands felt new life in the controls with our cargo of hate smashing down to its hellish purpose. My eyes climbed back up to the high box, to the number two man, left wing of the element.

Now it was a scene detached, a moving picture upon the screen of my windshield. The dark olive-drab of the bomber was spewing bright red soiled by ugly black that marked its course across a faultless blue curtain. Still the bomber reached, agonizingly, for more altitude. A futile gesture, prolonging the pain. The only sound effects for the bitter drama was the drone of our engines and the soft crack of flak still spattering too damned close.

Suddenly the picture, hellishly fascinating, assumed its true identity. There were ten kids burning up inside that aerial blast furnace. Flames were blocking the exits for any still alive. As from a distance, I could hear myself screaming into my oxygen mask, "My God, my God, my God, my *God!*" I was strapped to my seat, chained to my own responsibility. Yet, it seemed that somehow I must be able to reach out across that clear expanse to help those poor devils. It seemed cruel to just sit there. To just hold formation, and to just sit there!

The flaming ship was now pitifully straining for altitude, left wing held high as though to save it from the inferno. The big ones die hard, I thought. Then this one died. At the top of the wingover, the doomed B-24 gave up. It didn't blow; it just melted apart. Like a bird caught by a blast of shot, the heavy parts fell first, and feathers of debris followed in a long string of smoking wreckage. Out of the feathers, a parachute took form.

Then blue sky returned. An empty, beautiful blue. Empty of a great bomber and ten men. Just like that. My divided consciousness became one again. My training hadn't provided for this interruption. I must become all pilot again.

Flak was thinning. I made a routine sweep of the instrument panel. It read well. Then my eyes locked. A wisp of smoke was drifting lazily up in front of them!

My first thought screamed, "My God, *we're* on fire!"

In the same instant, I forced my vision to follow the smoke to its source. It was my hands! It was not smoke. Steam streamed up from the fur-lined gloves that I preferred over the electrically heated standard issue. In the subzero atmosphere, sweat had soaked through the leather palms and it evaporated as steam.

We had finally found our war. And I had found fear.

Into my crowded thoughts leaped one of the great reasons that I had chosen the Army Air Force. "Either I'll come back in one piece, or I won't come back at all." This was the way I wanted it. This was the way I had wanted it before I had met up with death high over Bernberg. But now, down deep inside my churning guts I knew why man—and woman—fight for life with every remaining breath. I knew now why my stoic grandmother, one-fourth Indian and being eaten up by a cancer inside her, wanted to live when she knew she was dying. "I am ready to meet my destination," she had said only a day before she begged to live—and died.

Now I wanted to live. At that moment, I would willingly give a leg just to know that I could make it home. My soul was not in my extremities. They would have to blast my heart out to get at my life. They could have any part of me, but not my life.

My knees were shaking. I jammed them against the rudder pedals. The shaking stopped.

It was to be the last time that I was to show or to feel any outward evidence of the fear that would become routine emotion. It was a part of my training that had been neglected. But now I was trained. Whatever part of me had resisted the transition to manhood was lost somewhere over Bernberg.

And we had prayed. What part God wanted in that gruesome mess only He knows. If He could hear our prayers above the sounds of hate, He would have had to make a fast decision to determine whether to answer in English or in German.

As the flak thinned out and we headed homeward, we wondered what had happened to the Royal Air Force. Not a friendly fighter was visible from thirty minutes before the target until we hit England. But we did see one of the unmarked '24's heading back toward Germany. It had been a big mission for Jack who had helped with much of the flying. The plane had flown mushy until the bombs had been dumped from her; she had given us a real workout. As Rauscher dug the flak that missed him out of the radar equipment, we discovered another hole in the left wing. It appeared to have come from one of the enemy fighters. With over six of the seven hours and thirty minutes on oxygen, we were beat. The sandwiches and Scotch whiskey were welcome as we gave our reports at interrogation by the intelligence officers of S-2. Our only casualty was Sergeant Schow. His electrical suit had shorted, and he had blistered burns on the inside of each elbow. Despite the pain, he didn't mention it until we were on the ground. He was sent to the hospital to have the burns treated.

We learned that the airplane which had gone down from our group was piloted by an officer on his twenty-third mission. Those near him said that he had tried to jettison his load through the bomb door when one of them failed to open. Normally, the weight of bombs would have ripped the door off, but this one held. Whether it was the flak I saw which set off the retained bombs, or whether the bombs themselves had exploded in the fuselage, the end result was the same.

One bit of good news came our way. We discovered that we had just completed our second mission. Upon the CO's recommendation, we had been credited with a mission for our first trip in the wing-heavy airplane.

Only twenty-three to go.

6

An easy access to the grave
  Yawns yearning e'er to foe or friend,
To call the cowards or the brave,
  For only God can guess the end.
But to that catastrophic call,
  If e'er my efforts lose the light,
I beg but one thing for my all—
  To find my own field for the fight.
                    From "A Pilot's Plea"

We stood down on April 12 while ground crews pasted our bombers back together. It was a welcome respite. The Bernberg mission had produced a marked effect on the entire crew. It took a bit of getting used to this abrupt transformation. Gone was the carefree attitude and the eagerness. Now I could better understand the faraway look in the eyes of the men we had met in the briefing room when we had taken our place on the firing line.

Beat-up bombers had concerned us with their unstable flying characteristics, fickle instruments and erratic superchargers. Hideous weather had thrown a scare or two into us. We had felt rather impersonally the impact of the war when the eleven bombers failed to return on the first mission in which we had a part.

But now we had tasted bitter broth from the hellish caldron of combat. The more vigorous emotions that had propelled us toward whatever glory there is in war had moved aside for a quiet fear that permeated our very beings. This is what I had seen in the eyes of men who were not unfriendly but who did not want to reveal the feelings so strong that they feared they might show. I began to understand the true definition of bravery.

The camera lens picked up some of this new emotion, this desperate sense of duty that crowded back the fear and left room for only empty smiles. A photographer from the base caught us together before we boarded our bomber late the next morning. This was a photo for home. We wondered if it might be the last.

We had reason for such wondering. The target was Schweinfurt, a long haul, a tough target. Many groups had been savagely ripped by the Luftwaffe for daring to attack the ball bearing plants so important to the German war machine. But we were after another airport. It was a big effort, and we again found ourselves with one of the bombers that had been tacked together with imagination and appeared to have been scheduled out of curiosity.

Time had ceased to exist, measured now in missions, and the date of April 13 didn't offer any mental hazard. The old B-24 provided enough real peril in her own right. The even dozen 500-pounders in her belly were too much for the old lady. I could feel it even when we taxied away from the dispersal area. She bucked too wildly at the brakes, and the overflow load of gasoline began to slop down into the bomb bay. I recalled two of the gunners up from the tail section to hold down the flight deck. Another was stationed with a fire extinguisher at the head of the bomb bay in the event a spark met up with that gasoline.

It was 10:30 A.M., the latest we had started away from the base of the 44th. We used all the runway. And as we staggered up to our meeting place, assembly was poor. We headed for the Belgian coast with little semblance of a formation. We would have to patch it up enroute. By the time we fought our way into position, number one supercharger had given up and oil was flowing badly from number two engine.

With full power, we were barely keeping with the formation. Then numbers two and three cylinder-head temperatures climbed to 275, dangerously high. I used cowl flaps in an attempt to cool the engines. The additional drag ate into our dwindling gas supply.

We had 17,000 feet at the coast of Belgium, but we were in serious trouble. Sick at heart with the decision I had to make, I told the crew of my plan.

"We're not going to make it again today. But we're not wasting this load." We had just been informed at briefing that it was now permissable to bomb any target of opportunity anywhere in Europe. Prior to that time, our orders were to get rid of our bombs over Germany in an emergency or try to hold them for the North Sea. So now I addressed myself to the bombardier. "Larry, you start looking for an airfield where we can dump this load. It is going to be tough without the bombsight, but we should be able to hit a field at this altitude."

I dropped below the formation and continued on under its protection while we checked the ground. About ten miles inside the continent, I made a 180 and turned back.

"There's a field off to our left, Larry. Let's try for it," I suggested. "You talk me over it."

Larry Davis' "Roger" indicated he understood. I pointed our nose in that direction. Since I could no longer see our intended target, I waited for the bombardier's directions.

"I think I see a better field," Larry finally came back. "Want to try it?"

"You call it," I advised. Then I concentrated on our heading and listened for instructions.

"Ten degrees right. A little more. Hold it. Hold it. A fraction left. Steady . . . steady . . . steady . . ."

"Can't do it!" Larry suddenly exclaimed. "Clouds in the way. I can't see well enough."

"Let's get out of here," the navigator suggested.

My better sense agreed with Dale Rauscher. But the

thought of again returning to base with nothing accomplished rankled. I rolled the bomber into a steep bank.

"We'll try it again," I told the crew, and shut my mind to the mumblings coming over the interphone. There was strong opposition. But it subsided when it was obvious that, regardless of the consequences, we were indeed going to make another pass.

The second run ended like the first. Cloud patches were building beneath us, and visibility was becoming more and more restricted. To the relief of the rest and my personal disgust, we headed for England. It would be much too risky to attempt another pass. There were no friendly fighters in sight, and we would be easy pickings if the Luftwaffe moved in on us.

As we headed out over the North Sea on Rauscher's heading for home, a P-47 fighter came in from eleven o'clock out of the growing haze over the water. It flew up off our left wing on a quartering angle that would take it behind us. I couldn't read any markings, and I called it out.

"There's a '47 coming up off our left. I can't read anything on it. It is probably ours, but keep an eye on it."

The fighter passed out of my sight to the rear. Cox picked him up at five o'clock, and reported. Then his voice changed.

"He's coming in on us!" George shouted.

I threw the ship into a sharp right bank, into the direction of the fighter's approach. Then I heard Cox's single 50-caliber take off. Immediately, Schow opened up from the tail turret. Sanders, in the top turret, was trying for him, but I threw the wing in his way. Then, as I righted the bomber, I heard Renfro join in from the left waist. A quick glance to the left showed the fighter flying level with us, several hundred feet out. But intermittent tracers were moving up on his tail from behind me.

"Cease fire!" I shouted. For seconds more, the firing continued as I continued to bellow into my throat mike. The firing stopped.

The P-47 slid off into the haze, its nose pointed toward

London. It was soon swallowed in the distance, and we could not mark whether it continued in that direction.

For long minutes, the only sound was the throbbing drone of our engines. Not a word was spoken. I would find out later why George Renfro was so slow in holding his fire. When he heard his buddies open up on the fighter, George made a dive for his gun. In the scramble, he lost his ear phones, and he couldn't hear my "Cease fire." As soon as they realized it, Cox and Reichert tackled him and pulled him from his gun.

My only thought now was that my gunners had fired on a P-47. P-47's were American airplanes, built and presumably flown by Americans. And three of my men had tried to finish this particular one off. Apparently my tone, when I stopped the show, didn't encourage conversation. Finally I broke the silence.

"Well, you guys, when we get back we'll have a class in aircraft identification."

Again there was a prolonged silence. Then Schow broke in from the tail turret.

"Sir, we *knew* it was a P-47. But he made a regular pursuit curve on us!"

"Then why in the hell didn't you knock him down?" I challenged.

"I don't know, sir. I had him right in there." There was both relief and disappointment in Schow's voice.

With the ice broken, the hubbub on the interphone renewed, and I felt better again. One of the first things I had insisted upon with this fine group of youngsters was that they report *everything* of any significance to me over the interphone. It was Rauscher's duty to mark down anything that might be of interest to S-2 when we returned. Some of the talk seemed to be and was superfluous. But, it was a way to let off nervous energy, and I knew at all times what was going on in the rear of the plane. And, more importantly, *around* the plane.

When I announced that we were going to land with our 6,000 pounds of heavy demolition bombs, murmurs over the interphone indicated that for the second time that day I had made an unpopular decision.

"Those bombs cost a dollar a pound, and I can't see wasting them," I explained. "Anyway, if they aren't armed, they aren't supposed to be able to go off even if we do drop one of them on the runway when we land."

There were a few more opinions offered which were somewhat to the left of center, but it was my decision. The men knew that theoretically I was right. But then there have been theories which have been blown sky high. I swung wide at our base to get a clean shot at the runway. With just enough power to slow our descent, I coaxed the old girl onto the concrete. She touched down gently, almost timorously, as though to apologize for the grisly ride she had given us, the *wherrp* of her tires no louder than a car sliding too close to the curb.

It took me some time to realize that it was the actual weight of the bomb load, as much as the delicate responsibility that rested on my handling, which made the landing so neat. Even my crew, not always impressed with my previous landings, said things that helped ease the pain of our second abortion.

But there was nothing to ease the obvious pain showing in the crew chief's face as he signaled us in to our dispersal area. Obviously we were bringing back a black mark on his record. I shut off the engines and marked up the number two for repair. Then I explained our problems to the chief. He listened politely to my full report, but I thought I detected a certain incredulity in his attitude, more of a resignation to the authority that flew his airplanes than a real belief that one of them could fail to perform with perfection.

The base was on standdown the next day. I gave the colonel a chance to hold a critique on the mission of the day before. Our group had made it to the target area and back without loss, but results were mixed. There were some rough spots in flying. Certain aspects of the group's air conduct were reviewed with an aim to improving future missions. It was interesting and helpful to be able to look back on a mission rather than to sweat one out for a change. However, there was one part of the critique that heated up my particular spot in the briefing room.

"We had one incident yesterday that I would like to talk about for a moment. One of our planes was unable to complete the mission, and the pilot turned back. There was nothing wrong in his turning back since the plane could not make the mission. We're not questioning his judgment on aborting. However, on the way back he did a 360 over the coast trying to find a target for his bombs. Of course, it is now permissible to drop anywhere on the continent if you can find a target."

The colonel was not mentioning any names.

"We commend the pilot for his eagerness, but we can't say as much for his judgment."

Well, after that, I needed some air. I took a ride to the dispersal area on my recently acquired bicycle. Bicycles were scarce. You had to wait until its owner was shot down or had finished his tour. Not many were finishing. But it wasn't necessary to wait too long for a bicycle. I wanted to check on our most recent failure.

"It's a good thing you brought her back, sir," the crew chief explained. "You had a bad crack in your oil line near the prop governor. You would never have been able to get her back—even if you made it to the target."

At least part of my judgment had been in good working order.

7

There is no bravery without fear,
Nor ever courage great alone.
But fools are fearless, though their stone
May sometimes mark a hero's bier.
                    From "About Bravery"

A .500 average may be fine in baseball, but not in bombing. We weren't the happiest bomber crew in the European Theater of Operations. We had logged a total of twenty hours and fifty minutes getting in two accredited missions out of four tries. Our war had covered five days.

It appeared that the weather or mechanical failure had a fifty-fifty chance of getting us before the Luftwaffe did.

Although much of the eagerness had gone out of us, it was replaced by a grim purpose to collect our twenty-five missions and get home. Down deep, fear gnawed a growing hole in our confidence that we would ever complete the required number. The unasked question of "Will you get it?" had been replaced with the more forbidding one of "When will you get it?"

Still, we were morbidly anxious to keep moving, and it was with a certain satisfaction that I found my name posted for the trip on the eighteenth of April. I had flown one practice mission over England and gathered one trip in the link trainer after the fiasco of the thirteenth.

There were two things which never showed on our flying records. One was the sometimes interminable waiting after we were roused from our warm sacks until word came for briefing. Another was the time spent on the ground after we were aboard our airplanes before the moment I stood on the brakes with all engines straining and called for "Close bomb doors." It was often a big chunk of day between touching bare feet down on the cold floor of our Nissen hut and turning loose the brakes for our takeoff roll. Even after the flare to start engines, it was a long time before we found our way from the dispersal area to the head of the runway. This was particularly true when we first started to fly combat and were near the last plane in line.

This latter situation was of some concern when we had a long one to fly. It took precious gasoline to keep our four fans turning for the taxi routine.

And the mission of April 18 was a long one. The usual groans accompanied the briefing officer's tracing of our proposed trip deep into Germany. It was to be another airfield near Brandenburg, about thirty miles southwest of Berlin itself. Further, we would make a sweep north across the North Sea and enter enemy territory about fifteen miles south of Denmark's border. Then we would swing down to the target, drop, and make a beeline for home. It sounded relatively simple—in the briefing room.

Our crew climbed inside the *Hornet's Nest*. From the time I nudged the engines into action, I had the feeling that we had finally been given a good airplane. At any rate, it was a considerable improvement over anything I had yet flown—particularly the *Wasp Nest*.

We slid in over Germany without incident after forming on course to save gasoline. Flak greeted us as soon as we came within range, and it continued to probe for us much of the way. However, it was generally to one side or the other. We were in no real danger most of the distance to the target. The lead navigator was doing a splendid job in picking his way through the flak fields.

However, as we approached the target, flak increased in

At Topeka, Kansas, in late February of 1944, the crew lines up with *Sweet Eloise* just before starting with the new B-24 Liberator Bomber for England via South America and Africa. *First row:* Lieutenants Dale E. Rauscher, navigator; Jay "Larry" Davis, bombardier and nose gunner; John "Jack" F. Emerson, co-pilot; Keith C. Schuyler, pilot. *Second row:* Sergeants Walter E. Reichert, ball turret gunner; Harry J. Schow, tail gunner; George N. Renfro, assistant engineer and left waist gunner; Leonard A. Rowland, radio man; George G. Cox, right waist gunner; William L. Sanders, engineer and top turret gunner.

Up for the fourth mission in four days, the strain of repeated trips aloft and five credited missions in 13 days shows on the faces of the crew when compared to the carefree photo taken at Topeka. This is *The Banana Barge* just before takeoff on a trip to Berlin which was washed out by weather. *Front row:* Rauscher, Emerson, Schuyler and Davis; *rear:* Reichert, Sanders, Renfro, Rowland, Schow and Cox.

"Guard" at Dakar, French West Africa, with *Sweet Eloise* before she had her name painted on the fuselage. Book is upside down.

I paid a GI seven bucks at Marrakech to paint the name on *Sweet Eloise* after I lettered it for him. They took her away from us as soon as we landed in Wales the next day.

Part of the crew guarding the base at Dakar comes to a salute, each in his own way, for my camera.

Had to lose at checkers near Dakar to get the village chief to take me fishing while we waited for repairs on an engine that was acting up crossing the South Atlantic.

One of the war-weary bombers that was sent to the battle of Casper, Wyoming, where new B-24 crews were trained. Standing in front of this one before a training flight are Rauscher, Emerson, Davis, Sanders and Schow.

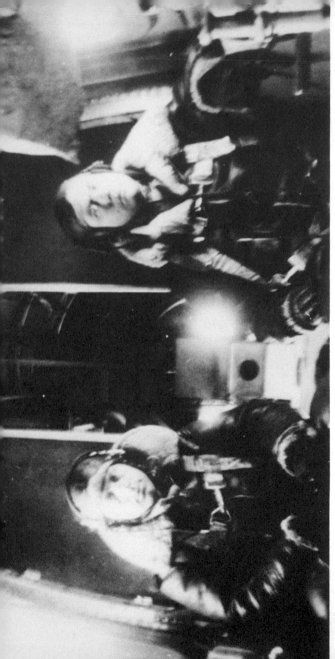

Cox and Schow fight the cold on one of the countless training missions before the crew was combat ready.

intensity and accuracy. The object of our bombs was another bastion in the Maginot line of airfields that guarded Berlin, and ground and air resistance was in proportion to its importance. We were forced into violent evasive action to avoid the black poppy fields that began to block our way.

Finally came that long moment that all bomber crews dreaded. The steady on-course line direct to the target, those hour-filled minutes when each pilot had to concentrate on holding his wing as close as possible to the waist window of the aircraft next to him, when evasive action was out until the plane lifted from the weight of bombs dropping from her bay. The seconds ticked off as black flak clusters floated at us from the aerial explosions ahead—until only a few separated the lead bombardier's thumb from his release.

Then, like the sudden fog of water on fire, we plunged into a solid cloud bank.

I strained my eyes to keep contact with our element leader. Nearly six hundred miles of low, thin, scattered clouds, at 20,000 feet, and now this! The thick gray stuff completely enveloped the formation. There was no chance to drop bombs with visibility cut off from the lead squadron. I had no way of knowing what might be beneath us. Other groups were homing in on our target. I clung to our element with the faint hope that we would come out close enough to the group to use our bombs. Even in the thick grayness, black blobs continued to burst so close that we could see their dark imprint within the mist.

After about eight minutes, we broke out amid complete pandemonium. Directly ahead were nine ships from our group. On all sides the Luftwaffe was mixing it with friendly fighters which had moved in over us at the target. Fortunately, there were no fighter attacks on our bombers. We had enough trouble of our own to supplement the heavy flak attack.

Even as I watched, four ships of the nine released their fifty-two 100-pound incendiaries. At the same time, our element leader, apparently confused, made almost a ninety-degree turn away from course. I headed for the protection of our main group, hoping that our fighters would keep the air clear for the maneuver.

We kept watching for the rest of our group to make the bomb drop. However, most had dumped their loads in the clouds. And when it appeared that we were on a course for home, I began to look for a target. Flak was becoming less a problem, but the extra gasoline needed to keep up with the homeward bound formation of empties was cause for real concern.

As a temporary measure, I called for bomb doors to be closed. I could feel and hear the hydraulic system at work to stitch up our open belly, but it seemed to be taking longer than usual. Finally, Larry called me.

"Keith, there's something wrong. I can't close the bomb doors! They're stuck halfway. See if you can move them."

I reached for the pilot's emergency handle. My efforts were only partly successful. I could feel the mechanism working, telegraphed through my cable release, but it had a sluggish feel.

"You moved them," Sanders called out, "but they're still not all the way open. I think the bombs will clear, though."

I slid to the side of the formation and asked Larry to find a target.

"When you see something ahead on course, talk me on to it," I said. "Then hit your toggle. Rauscher, if it doesn't work, pull the salvo handle. If that doesn't work, call out and I'll try to dump them from here."

I followed Larry's directions as he headed us toward a burning factory that some other group had pounded on a diversionary mission. "It must be an important target," he rationalized. "A little more to the right, just a hair more . . . hold it." I froze on the heading. "Get ready, get ready . . ."

Then Larry shouted. "No!" I already had hold of the salvo handle. Rauscher's immediate, "No luck!" was my signal. I heaved mightily on the cable-attached handle.

Nothing happened.

I swung back to the formation, shoving our manifold pressure higher than I liked to gain position.

"Jack," I urged, "call the lead ship and ask them if they can slow it down a bit."

"We've got to get those doors moved," Larry cut in. "Apparently they are in a position that cuts off all the release mechanism."

"We'll check it out," Sanders offered and climbed down from his top turret. Rowland got up from his radios at Sanders' touch on his shoulder, and both of them donned walk-around oxygen bottles. We had dropped down to about 18,000 feet, but we were still much too high for natural breathing. Then Jack switched to interphone.

"Group lead says they are going about as slow as they dare to hold formation," he reported. "But they'll try to drop it back a little."

I knew the problem. It was necessary for the formation to fly considerably faster than would be required for a single plane. Flying too close to stalling speed was extremely dangerous. If the lead suddenly cut back too much, those cutting their throttles to keep from overrunning the ship ahead risked stalling out. A stalled-out airplane would be risky enough in itself, but it would also create a hazard to other planes in the formation.

Meanwhile, Sanders and Rowland had gone out on the catwalk to check the bomb doors. If their oxygen supply ran out or cut off, there was nothing beneath them but the narrow steel path to the waist and 18,000 feet of subzero atmosphere. The cold was an additional hazard as they searched the bomber's interior.

It was now slightly easier to keep with the formation, but I took more than one worried look behind me at the tall gas gauges while keeping an eye on the two men. Rowland went to his radio table and came on interphone.

"We've found the trouble. An empty cartridge casing is stuck in the roller channel on the right bomb door. Sanders is trying to work it loose with a pair of pliers."

A few minute later, Sanders himself called to Davis.

"Lieutenant Davis, I think it will work now. Give it a try."

The groan and roll of the bomb doors moving freely up and down was sweet music a moment later.

"Okay, we'll try it again," I called to Rauscher. "We'll just salvo the whole load as soon as possible so that we can get these doors closed." Between the bombs and the drag we were losing about ten miles per hour that I had to make up with extra gas consumption. I made a quick choice. Ahead, and almost directly on course, a train was moving through a small town. "You try the salvo handle, Rauscher. But, if it doesn't work, holler out and I'll try it from here."

I was already lining up on the target when I got his "Roger." Then I asked him for the wind and eased a bit into it. With no bomb sight, it would be mostly guess work. Then things looked about right.

"Salvo!"

"No go!" called Rauscher. I jerked my salvo handle.

I listened to the crew as they followed the bombs. "They look good . . ." "No, too strong . . ." "Maybe, maybe . . ." "There they go!"

"You were just about one hundred yards past the target," Larry said. "We blew up a patch of woods just past the town."

I would forever wonder what the result would have been if the bombs had gone away on Rauscher's attempt to salvo. Would the brief separation in time between his try and mine have made the difference between a miss and a direct hit?

We slid back into formation and continued on toward the coast. Implications of our recent attempt and the new feeling of confidence engendered by having everything again running smoothly gave me a chance to contemplate the feelings of those far beneath us.

It was a rotten business, this bombing of anything that looked like a target. The great saturation bombings of cities was yet to come. But, the order to take any target of opportunity if necessary was forerunner to the raids which smashed cities like Nuremberg, Berlin, and Hanover. It brought a disquieting feeling that had not been anticipated when we first planned for war.

What of those below who had permitted their leaders to order such bombings in England? How did they now feel about having their homes destroyed as an incident to our honest effort to bomb military targets? And now, how must they feel as bombs dropped anywhere from stray airplanes or groups which found their primary target obscured and had to empty their racks to make it home from the deep penetrations?

True, it was an impersonal thing to fly above even the smoke of flaming homes and factories; above the explosions which would bruise a man's face purple from concussion alone; above the frantic cries and screams of women and children caught in this horrible thing known as modern war. I felt my part in this great sin. I knew I shared it no more than the streetcar conductor in San Francisco, the farmer in Idaho, or the workers assembling tanks in the factory from which I enlisted in the Army Air Force Cadet program. But even my part carried a weight on my conscience that was inconsistent with my feelings toward all people.

Then I thought of Coventry. I thought of the black holes in the beautiful city of Norwich that we passed on the way to the cinema the one night we were able to get away from our base. And I felt better. I felt better not because I felt any less guilty. But I had reached out and found the excuse that man ever seeks to assuage his conscience.

Our gasoline tanks showed a total of only four hundred gallons when we crossed the Dutch coast. Our troubles had been costly in fuel. As soon as we were far enough away from land to minimize any chance of being accosted by enemy fighters, I had Jack get permission to break formation.

We headed straight for our base to land ahead of the group to avoid any chance of being delayed. Our gasoline supply was not critical; but it was far from comfortable. I chalked up eight hours of flight time on the log.

It was another mission. But, for all our long hours in the air, we may have hit no more important target than a rabbit.

8

Oh God,
My soul I ever offer Thee:
My body pledged to feed the fight;
But in that pledge goes all of me;
My trust that what I do is right.

Impunity I cannot ask
From the horrors of the line;
But courage for the coming task—
And strength, Oh God, may it be mine.
From "Battle Prayer"

So now we had credit for three missions.

You don't start counting in earnest on the first few tries. It is the big challenge getting started in the great sport of war that erases statistics. Until suddenly you discover that it is more of a job than a challenge, and more of a war than a sport. Then you start counting. Not hours or days, or even months behind you. You start counting steps forward that lead you away from the conflict.

The merry Crusade that starts with shining armor, sweet kisses and proud tears starts to pick up some of the dust of the road. And you discover that there is blood in the dust. The dust and the blood begin to stain the shiny armor, and the man inside feels the heat and the blood and the dust. Some of it clouds his vision of the Holy Grail. He thinks more often of home.

But pricks of pride and conscience urge him forward. He rides the well-trained steed, trained to move ahead, and knows no consequence if his food is good and on time. His arms and legs move, independent of his longing. They make him do well or die; they make him do well— and die.

Three missions; twenty-two to go. The figure takes on a different perspective when you write it out, becomes less a statistic and more a real barrier than a mere figure of twenty-two. Like love and hate and anger, it assumes a dimension to be reckoned with. But you must have fought your very steed, you must have battled weather, frustration, fear, even the enemy, before you start counting the steps toward home that lead you straight into the heart of the flame and smoke.

You begin to wonder if the feeble results of your great effort make you indeed a soldier. You compare the cost in sweat and training that brought you this far to the results you have attained. Has your talent for killing been wasted on smoke trails of engines that don't even properly burn the great volume of gasoline required for five attempts; five attempts that have so far only delivered bombs once to a target properly? Then you think of those who smashed and burned themselves against the hillsides and mountains at home just trying for this chance to succeed. You think of those who flew with you who never made it over an intended target. These are dead, or crippled, or in any event lost to the effort. You still have a chance to do *something*. You want to do it with every fiber that holds you together. But now you are afraid. You have seen the blood in the dust.

April 19, 1944.

The squadron CO let us sleep until 6:30 A.M.

The pointer went halfway and south of a direct line to Berlin. Another airfield. This one is near Gutersloh, just northeast of the Ruhr Basin. There is bound to be plenty of flak. But the target is somewhat short of the main concentration of fighters around Hanover which guards the corridor from East Anglia to Berlin.

Our bomb load was an even dozen 500-pound heavy demolition bombs. Three tons—a fairly weighty load for the nearly seven-hour trip. For, we must stay north, above the heaviest flak concentrations, before heading south to our intended bulls-eye.

Sergeant Renfro is grounded with a touch of frostbite on one ear. A Sergeant Nicholson introduced himself at the plane, and he was assigned George's left waist gun.

My wrist watch read something past ten o'clock before we became airborne, and I searched out the all-too-familiar Purple Heart corner of the formation. My assignment was on the left wing of the low element in the bottom box, a co-pilot's delight with work easiest to handle from the right seat. Flak was light as we crossed the Zuider Zee to cut over the Netherlands. At the IP our sections split to make two distinct bombing runs. Overhead, P-51's, P-47's, and P-38's cut spider webs that challenged the Luftwaffe—a challenge that went unanswered.

Our bombing run was bordered with flak which crowded in from both sides. Although it came quite close, none of our ships were taking hits as we moved in on the target. Bombs straddled the airfield well. And as we moved away, flak continued to erupt from cities along our course, heavy, but more as though in warning than in intention. Jack provided welcome relief on the controls throughout much of the trip.

We took a direct course for home, crossing northern Belgium with little more than nuisance attention from the ground batteries. And it was here that we saw one of the proudest sights of the air war.

B-24's and B-17's in long lines thundered past on their uncompleted errands to the heart of Germany. At least five hundred of them passed within sight. The scene they presented was as much a source of pride and confidence to those of us on the way home as it must have been of consternation and dread to those for whom their bombs were intended.

Then we landed. I marked down six hours and forty-five minutes flying time for what had been one of our longest and by far the easiest of any trip to that date. What hell the other groups were stirring up as we stretched our muscles beside our airplanes, only the news reports would bring to us. But for us this had been a milk run. This time we had justified our presence in the war. The job was done, and neatly.

So now it was four. This war wasn't so bad after all. My name was on the bulletin board for the next day.

Now we were listed with the 67th Squadron. We didn't mind the shift. In fact, it meant better accommodations, squared-off stucco buildings in ugly camouflage outside and pleasantly painted walls of beige inside. What we would not realize for several days was the fact that we were again replacements. Our names again went on the bottom of every list.

We weren't given too much time to think about such things as promotions or raises in pay when the morrow held so many question marks. But we were enough concerned to be curious as to when our presence and efforts would be recognized. Promotions had slowed considerably. Previous crews had frequently moved up a notch just before or upon arrival in England. The latest scuttlebut indicated that the magic five-mission mark would bring the long awaited jump in rank for the entire crew.

Despite the listing on the bulletin board, chances of our getting in a fifth mission the next day were being washed away by low clouds and rain. It was so miserable that I let a cat that had been whining around the barracks in out of the damp cold. The rain had reduced to a chill drizzle by six o'clock when I got up to let out the cat.

The weathermen, who we suspected made their decisions by flip of a coin or drawing from a stacked deck, must have passed the word shortly after. At ten-thirty we learned that we were alerted.

"You'll like this one," the briefing officer assured us. "The Jerries are building heavy installations which we think are rocket pens. And we've spotted a number of them just southeast of Calais, in France. You will only be over enemy territory for a few minutes. You will be carrying a full load—eight 1,000-pound bombs. These installations are well protected with heavy concrete. We want to try to blast through them.'' We didn't know it then, but it was infamous V-1 rocket launching sites we were after. It would be nearly two months until the belated "Crossbow" barrage of flying bombs were to terrorize London.

It was a different from usual atmosphere as we gathered for the pilot's briefing. Everything pointed to a milk run. "Schuyler, you will fly left wing on the lead ship of the last flight over the target." The warning given at the general briefing was repeated. "You won't be over it long, but flak will be heavy. Get in and get out!" Assembly was good as we grabbed altitude over the North Sea.

As though to emphasize importance of the target, we could see a heavy volume of flak picking at the groups ahead of us as we approached the coast of France. It was accurate, too damned accurate. And size of the puffballs indicated 128-mm guns. One ship from the group ahead smashed into the ground and oblivion as bombs and gasoline sent a great cloud of flame and debris skyward. We raced a layer of clouds to the target.

The clouds won. For, as we swung in over our assigned area, the storm front below us blotted out vision of the ground. We watched for the drop, but the lead held his bombs. Dutifully, we clung to the squadron lead as he headed back toward the North Sea. Anti-aircraft guns continued to reach for us and a number of our group was collecting shrapnel.

"Put the pins back in," I called as soon as it was certain that we would not be dropping this trip. With only eight bombs aboard, it wouldn't take long to disarm our deadly load. By reinserting wires in the nose, action of the little propellers, which would bring the fuse in contact with the high explosive charge, would be prevented. According to tech orders, the propeller had to make so many turns before the bomb could be exploded. A hard landing could jar a bomb loose. But bombs could not read tech orders.

The manual did not contain the frequent prayers offered as further insurance to augment safety features of a missile built for destruction. Nobody had ever been able to report failure of a prayer.

Smoke began to pour from a plane in the squadron on our right. Flak had smashed through the bomb bay to sever the oxygen supply and electrical connections. The bomber dropped away and jettisoned its load. Crewmen managed to overcome the fire. It was the last mission for the pilot, and he headed home alone on a direct course.

This time my crew was silent as I swung wide for a careful approach with our 8,000-pound load. As with lightning, we would never hear the thunder if one of our bombs broke the rules, but landing with a load of steel-encrusted TNT could never become a pleasant habit. Our prayers worked.

As we ducked out of the bomb bay, somebody yelled, "Hey, we're heroes! We get the air medal!" It was the first that anyone realized that we now have five accredited missions as a crew. All but Cox and Renfro, who had each missed a mission, had the required minimum for the medal. More importantly, we were a fifth of the way home.

Weariness worked me over as I pounded out the usual nightly letter to Eloise. The pace was beginning to tell in actual physical fatigue. I was only mildly interested when I heard the loudspeaker in the next barracks blare out, "Red alert! Red alert!" Jerry was paying us a return visit.

From the coast came the sounds of air raid sirens moaning and the *krump-krump* of ack-ack guns. Within minutes, area artillery began to blast holes into the night and into our sleep. Off and on all night the British probed the now clear sky for members of the Luftwaffe. Finally, even the guns could not deny us the sleep we were needing more and more.

Wham! Wham! Just before daylight a German plane came tearing across the field, machine guns blazing and 20 mm's popping unpleasantly. Then the two big explosions.

One cannon shot hit a gas truck and did some damage

without starting a fire. Machine gun bullets went through one barracks but no one was hit. The bombs were more successful. Both landed in a trash pile and set it ablaze. Fortunately, the fire did not attract any more enemy planes as approaching daylight sent the Krauts back across the North Sea.

The same good weather that invited the Germans to England made it fairly certain that we would be making our fourth mission in as many days. But the call for briefing did not come until 10:30 A.M.

9

Each hero harks the hellish heed
Of his talent's course to coffin,
And mystic motives spurn the speed
To the end that comes so often.
From "An Airman's Plea"

Strangely enough, we now felt more a part of the 44th
Bomb Group. Maybe it was a hint of pride that now
claimed a place in our collective chest alongside the routine fear. Many didn't make five missions. And there was
that possible promotion.

We needed whatever lift was available when the inevitable map came flapping down on April 21. We were assembled for our fourth briefing in four days. The pointer
reached and reached and reached—then it settled on Berlin. I heard my own moan join the chorus. I had just
enough left of whatever it took to join the ripple of laugh-
ter that swept the room on the heels of our ludicrous performance a moment earlier. Nevertheless, the black
apprehension which settled over the group made the laugh-
ter seem as ludicrous as the affected groan of pain.

"This is a big one," the briefing officer announced. "A
few of you made the trip before, so you know it can be
done." His words were more defensive than assuring.

"You'll have fighter cover most of the way. But we can't do much for you over the target."

Reports from the meteorologists were not overly comforting. "The weather is a bit unsettled west of us. But we think we can give you clear sailing. You'll be bombing at 20,000 feet, and this should keep you well over anything you meet in the way of weather on the trip."

Briefing had started at 10:30 A.M., but it was well after lunch when we were called for takeoff. I shoved a few extra packs of cigarettes in my knee pockets. The old-timers had tipped us off that a downed flier could buy more with cigarettes than with money. Anyway, it was a matter of preference. German cigarettes were supposed to be terrible.

It was not that we didn't have money. The plastic-covered escape kits we carried had an assortment of bills that could be used in an attempt to buy freedom or some of the necessities which might otherwise be denied prisoners. In addition to the money, our kits provided such things as a compass, maps, fishing tackle, and other odds and ends of emergency needs.

One thing I had carried because it had been issued to me, I discovered was not favored by many fliers. My new squadron CO, Mormon by faith, brought up the subject as I was heading out to meet truck transportation to the dispersal area.

"Schuyler, I see you are carrying your forty-five." I looked down at the semi-automatic pistol which was standard sidearm issue. I had worn it as a matter of course on each mission. "Any particular reason?"

The question caught me off balance. It had never occurred to me not to wear it.

"No. I thought we were supposed to carry it."

"Well, it is entirely a matter of choice. But, well, most of us kind of look at it this way. If you get knocked down, you have every right to defend yourself and to try to get away. It might even be the difference between getting captured and getting back through the underground. However, if you do knock off a Kraut or two, the next guy to get shot down may get a warm reception. We hear that so far the Germans are treating downed fliers pretty good for the most part.''

I suddenly felt that the gun made me look ostentatious. It was a bit embarrassing. But hell, I was supposed to be a soldier, too. The captain, noting my discomfiture, grinned.

"Some of the boys wear them. One co-pilot has been shooting at fighters with his."

I put the gun back in my locker. Anyway, I was glad to shuck any nonessential gear. After donning coveralls, electrically heated flying suit, flying boots, flak vest, Mae West life preserver, parachute, headphones, throat microphone, helmet, goggles, oxygen mask, and gloves, a gun that you would hesitate to use would be excess weight. Although I had qualified as expert the one time I had used the gun in training, it had definite limitations.

All the men wore essentially the same gear. One exception was our parachutes. Back packs for bomber use were just coming into their own, but issue was limited to airplane commanders and co-pilots. The rest of the men wore harnesses adapted to chest packs. Getting in and out of turrets and various other duties about the airplane made the chest type chutes more practical. However, it was a more risky business. It only took seconds to snap the chute fast to the rings on the harness, but if the bomber went into a sudden and fatal maneuver, there was a chance that anyone not wearing his would never get the chance to fasten it. Consequently, each of the men wore his compact umbrella whenever possible. Sergeant Walter E. Reichert was the lone exception when he was at work. There just wasn't room for both him and the parachute in the ball turret slung under our belly. In an emergency, he would have to emerge from the turret, snap on the chute, and bail out.

It was approaching 2 p.m. when I climbed into the truck with the last of the men heading for the dispersal areas. Riding with me was a Lieutenant Hovens. He had arrived just recently, and this would be his second mission. Yet, in the brief time he had been on the base, we had struck up one of these quick friendships that I had found rare even among those with much more time to acquire acquaintances. Not that I had any special claim, for Hovens was an outgoing individual, the nice kid from the small-town prototype. He still had the same eager exuberance that was typical of new pilots and crews. He reminded me so much of the way I had felt so long ago when we started out thirteen days before. Moreover, he treated me with the respect due experienced pilots and asked questions that I had been asking almost two full weeks ago.

His last words, as he jumped from the truck, were, "Good luck, Schuyler; see you tonight."

My mood matched the darkening skies as I found our transportation for this long hop, the *Banana Barge*.* The old *Wasp Nest* was probably being stitched back together after she had nearly left us in the trees a few days before.

"She's a good ship," the crew chief assured me. But the name didn't excite much enthusiasm for a trip to Berlin—*Banana Barge*.

I couldn't help remembering back to the old turret lathe I had been assigned on my last job before enlisting in the Aviation Cadets. Nobody wanted it, and when I managed to get the required production of shafts for light army tanks out of it, they kept me on it. Nevertheless, I was never able to match the production of the other machines around me. Despite the crew chief's optimism, I doubted that the planes we were being assigned would ever be able to match the performance of the newer B-24's that were gradually replacing our beat-up bombers.

This time I took no chances. Although we were only carrying 240 light fragmentation bombs, I had full takeoff

---

*The *Banana Barge*, piloted by Irving Guran, was lost on May 12, 1944, after she was hit in the No. 2 engine by flak on a mission to Zeitz, German. She was last seen disappearing down into the haze with the No. 2 engine on fire. (From the book, *History of the 68th Squadron, 44th Bomb Group*.)

manifold pressure on all four engines before turning her loose. We lifted off with room to spare.

As soon as wheels and flaps were up, I turned her over to Jack. We had a long trip ahead of us, and I wanted to conserve my own energy as well as that of the *Banana Barge*. Our assignment in the formation was fighters' fancy, outside in the high box. And, few formations made it to Berlin and back without some attention from the Luftwaffe.

A light drizzle was falling as we left the field and climbed toward the clouds which appeared to be moving in fast. At 3,000 feet, we entered a thick layer of stratus clouds. At 19,000 feet we were just about to break out, and I took over the controls to look for our formation.

It was a moment or two before I realized that we were not quite making it into the sunlight which occasionally peeked in on us for a fleeting glance. Then I realized that the controls were getting sluggish; the ship felt as though she wanted to stall. My eyes flashed to the instrument panel. Power settings were slightly above normal, but now the airplane began to swing wildly. I was losing control!

Then the thought struck me—ice. A quick check of the wings confirmed my suspicion. The leading edge was covered with ice! Jack turned on the de-icer boots, and the heaving rubber covering the front of the wings began to crack the stuff away. We finally staggered into the sunlight, but much of the ice still clung to the wing despite action of the boots. I had to hold higher power settings than I liked to keep above the clouds. I began to search for *our* group.

Bombers, both '17's and '24's, were milling about in all directions. All of my crew strained for a sight of our group. But, condensation trails from the hundreds of airplanes were adding another 1,000 feet or so of artificial clouds to restrict visibility. It was another meteorological mess. I prayed for a recall. We were using up too much gasoline just trying to stay above the ice-forming clouds. Berlin! My God! After this!

Then it came. Orders crackled through on the secret and

seldom used radio to abandon the mission. All of us breathed a great sigh of relief. There were too many strikes against us to hope for a happy outcome of this one.

I had no desire to drop back down into those beautiful but dangerous clouds, and I headed out over the North Sea. A hole about thirty-five miles off the coast finally opened for us. We dropped down fast, anxious to get to warmer air, but the speed and moisture brought more ice. The rudders froze fast. I kicked the pedals desperately to free them. With reluctance they finally came loose and returned full control. As we at last leveled off in the warmer air, even the ice on the wings let go, and I gratefully headed back on instruments for home. My hope was that our fast descent would take us below the heavy traffic in the thick clouds and lessen the chance of smashing another airplane.

We kept the bombs in our racks and slid carefully onto the runway—damned glad to be on the ground again! Four hours and forty-five minutes we had fought the other enemy, and once again we had won. I marked down one-thirty for instrument time. This would not even count as a mission, for our battle had been over England.

Then I heard about Hovens.

He had lost his battle. Somewhere in that wet and freezing maelstrom of gray death, it was believed that his plane had collided with a B-17 which had wandered from its pattern into that of the 44th. His bomber exploded before it hit the ground. Rumors were rampant that several other ships had also been lost in a similar manner.

Each group of the many concentrated near The Wash in East Anglia had a definite pattern to fly under instrument conditions. And the patterns were so closely graphed that any deviation invited disaster. Disaster had struck. Without a shot being fired, the 8th Air Force had paid dearly for the meteorological miscalculation.

Those who paid most dearly had not even the satisfaction of going down fighting. Like a foot soldier smashed into the mud by one of his own tanks, these airmen were consumed in the bowels of a storm that allied itself with the enemy.

Mars laughed as souls of the unjustly condemned cried out against the storm while their remains fell in bits on the land they tried so hard to defend. Back home the newspapers would tell of the heroic deaths.

What a hell of a way to die!

10

—We seek them in the night; o'er moor and lea;
To where they press the sky back from the sea.
                              From "Elusive Horizons"

For the fifth day in a row, my name was up for the mission.

But it was a good day. The first news that greeted me was a report that Hovens had somehow escaped the mid-air collision. In some miraculous fashion, both he and his co-pilot were blown clear of the wreckage and they were able to open their parachutes. It was said, however, that all his other crewmen had been killed.

Neither Hovens nor his co-pilot escaped completely. The co-pilot sprained his ankle on landing. Hovens, according to our report, had landed in a tree with a broken left ankle. He fell from the tree and fractured his spine. But both were expected to recover in a hospital on another base.

We had plenty of time for loafing and for our briefing. The 44th was to be part of a new experiment. This time we were briefed to land in the dark, and takeoff would not be until late afternoon.

Disquieting news was drifting back from the continent, the briefing officer informed us. There were reports that the Germans were beginning to machine-gun airmen when they were descending in parachutes. Others had been pitchforked by farmers. Civilians in cities had killed some others being taken to prison camps.

This did not encourage any enthusiasm as the target was outlined. It would be the railroad marshaling yards at Hamm, on the northern edge of the famed Ruhr Valley, one of the most heavily defended spots in Europe.

"We can't even estimate the number of flak guns you will encounter," the briefing officer informed us. "We can only guarantee you that there will be plenty. However, you may miss seeing fighters. The Luftwaffe has not been especially active in that area the past few days. It will be completely dark when you return. We have alerted the ground crews, and they have been instructed to handle things. When you finish your landing roll, a jeep with a light will pick you up and guide you to your dispersal area. You have all that night flying, and this should be no different than anything you have had back in the states."

The briefing officer caught himself up a moment.

"Well, yes, there might be a difference. The Jerries have been following some of our bombers back, so keep your crews on the ball. They sometimes hit a plane as it is coming in for a landing. But you might find them anywhere on the way back."

Again I was assigned a position nearer the front of the formation. We were moving up to where it was a bit more comfortable from the standpoint of flak, but we were back in the *Wasp Nest*. The old girl was behaving a bit more to my liking, but I did not trust her completely. Superchargers were a constant source of trouble with many B-24's, and those on engines of the *Wasp Nest* had been particularly troublesome. Designed to maintain the efficiency of the airplane in the thin air at high altitudes, they were an absolute necessity. If one of them did not work properly, it put an additional strain on the remaining engines and cut dangerously into the gasoline supply.

It was 4 P.M. when we rolled down the runway to participate in the "experiment."

With the sun behind us, it was a new and pleasant sensation to cross the North Sea without squinting into the glare. Instead of burning us with bright rays, magnified by windshield glass, the sun splashed itself across the instrument panel and bathed the formation from behind. Although these were merely plus values to add to whatever the higher-ups had in mind when planning the late takeoff, the immediate effect was all to the good. However, sitting in the back of each of our minds was an unknown specter wearing a black mask, waiting to be reckoned with as soon as the sun went down.

True, we *had* flown numerous night training flights back in the States. We had bombed the Wyoming prairie repeatedly. But we did not do much formation flying after daylight hours. It was too damned dangerous for planes and crews. The British, masters of night bombing, sent their Lancasters and Stirlings and Halifaxes singly over the target and brought them back the same way.

My thoughts went back to one night over Wyoming when we flew in weather far below zero with defective cabin heaters. The crewmen huddled, each in his own frigid position, with only Larry and me alert to the job of dropping our blue 100-pound practice bombs on the lighted ground target. As we moved onto the bombing run, I turned controls of the airplane over to Larry's bombsight. Boring through the night, elevators, ailerons, and rudder magically responded to Larry's knobs on the bombsight. I divided my attention between the instruments and the black outside. Then it happened!

A red light loomed out of the night directly on our right wing. For a tiny fraction of a second, I was mesmerized by the light. Then my thumb hit the emergency release on the steering column and I rolled the bomber wildly to the left. Another B-24, with frozen crew and the bombardier "flying" by bomb sight, had been converging at the same altitude and air speed on the same target!

Oh well, at least we would be bombing Hamm in daylight. And it stayed light aloft much longer than it did on the ground, up out of the shadow of earth's contour and the stubble of buildings and trees and the mounds of mountains. As we sliced away mile after mile of sky, the mission was going close to perfect. Navigators were doing a good job of keeping us away from heavy flak. The stuff coming up was well to one side and below our altitude. Then I received a call from Larry.

"Keith, the heat has gone off in my gloves. My hands are getting numb."

I acknowledged the call with a simple "Roger." Larry's voice had held no excitement of urgency. He had merely reported a fact. However, the implications of his announcement were serious. Not only was there a strong possibility that his hands could freeze long before we dropped to warm air, we would have to employ alternative arrangements to drop our bombs. I *could* get Reichert up to man the nose turret. But there was the bombardier himself to consider. Larry knew as well as I that there could be no turning back; one man's hands or one man's life could not stand in the way of delivering the deadly gray load in the guts of our B-24.

Suddenly the pleasant flight over Germany was no longer pleasant. In deference to the plight of the bombardier, the interphone had gone silent. All were busy with their thoughts. I wondered if they expected me to take some action. Larry called again. "Bombardier to pilot." I acknowledged, hoping that he was out of trouble.

"My feet are getting numb now."

Again Larry's voice was even and matter-of-fact. We had flown a long way together. If something didn't happen soon, it would be our last as a complete crew. That something would have to exclude any thought of turning back. It was just that simple, that terribly simple. Long moments passed, more miles, then Sergeant Bill Sanders broke the renewed silence. "Engineer to bombardier." Lieutenant Davis acknowledged.

"Sir, have you checked your fuse box?"

More agonizing moments passed as we shared a common thought. Now who would ever expect to look in a fuse box to find the cause of an electrical failure? The simplicity of Sanders' suggestion was not lost on anyone. We had just never had an electrical suit go out before. It was probably fortunate that none of us had to face the other at that moment. Davis called me shortly.

"Everything's okay now. I had a fuse blown."

Our collective sigh of relief was short-lived. Ahead lay the thickest field of flak that we had yet seen. The sky was literally plastered with it for miles. And our course led directly into it. Airplanes were thick among the yet distant black freckles, and smoke coming up from below indicated that we were far from being first over this target.

Except for the nearness of the unbelievable barrage from ground guns, our bomb run was uneventful. Then, at almost the moment of release, another group slid in beneath us. There was only one thing to do, and we did it. The lead ship started a wide 360° sweep directly over the dreaded Ruhr Valley. We had only heard of the "flak alley" that constituted German defense of the heavily industrialized Ruhr, but now we were seeing it. What we saw appeared to be almost a carpet of flak bursts, the kind of stuff you can "get out and walk on." In addition to the miracle of so many guns concentrated in such an area was the unexplained fact that we were apparently flying safely through the stuff.

As we again lined up for the bomb run, doors still gaping open from the abortive first try, the entire target area seemed to be a mass of explosions. Then our own contribution went whistling down to further enrage the elements.

This is the way the newspapers described it:

The Forts and Libs, with escorts of P38's, 47's, and 51's from the Eighth and Ninth Air Forces, were striking in very great strength for the fourth time in five days when they went to Hamm Saturday. With good visibility, the heavies heaped explosives on the railway yards here which are rated at a capacity of 10,000 cars daily. Heavy damage was done to the Hamm yards, photographs showed, with bombs striking all along a three-mile stretch of tracks and switching trains. Fires, possibly from tank cars, spread after the attack, and the main station and repair shops also seemed to have been hit solidly, according to the photos. Steel works near the yards were hit, and fires were still burning there as the bombers turned away.

"Close bomb doors" finally came and we turned away from the target, flak still reaching—bursting, bursting. A loud explosion suddenly erupted on the flight deck and bits of glass stung the right side of my face. Something hit my right side!

I felt no severe pain, but I was afraid to look at Jack. For a hellish instant, when I forced my eyes his way, I thought I saw a wide rip in the left arm of his flying suit. But as we continued turning, the mirage, created by the sudden bath of sinking sun which swept across the flight deck and my imagination, disappeared. I followed Jack's gaze. There was a ragged hole in the glass canopy about six inches over his head. There were two more holes in our right wing which wouldn't reveal themselves until we landed.

But there was still the radioman, Rowland, at his table behind Emerson, the only other man on the flight deck, to be considered. He had heard the explosion despite his earphones. His reassuring grin told me that he was okay.

Sergeant Leonard Rowland, of Portland, Oregon—the quiet one. With his ears glued to the mysterious noises coming over his headset, and only his dials and the side of the fuselage for company, he was in another world than ours. Only when something unusual happened could he be aware of the other members of the crew or the working of the airplane itself. He was our emergency man, and a mighty good one.

As we moved away from the target area, a bomber from another group dropped out of formation with a burning number two engine. It dropped behind our view and to whatever fate that time, that day, that mission had in store for it. Then George Renfro, our enthusiastic Texan, called from the left waist.

"There's a red plane taking off from a field down there!"

I acknowledged the call as usual. But I wondered absently just what it was that Renfro actually saw. No red planes had been reported in all of Germany to my knowledge. Yet I never wanted to discourage any of the men from reporting anything unusual, or even usual, that they saw. We had started the reporting routine back in training; this was no time to take anything lightly. Not more than a few minutes later, Renfro came through with another report that strained my credulity.

"Here comes that red plane. He's firing rockets at the formation!"

"Roger, Renfro," I acknowledged. I wondered what Rauscher was thinking as he entered this one in his log. We had heard rumors that the Germans had built some kind of airplane with jets instead of propellers, but the time between takeoff and approach to the formation for this one just didn't add up to anything of which I was aware. Oh well, a short time before I had thought Jack was badly hurt when he didn't have a scratch on him. We were all probably getting a little flak-happy.

Then somebody called out to report another '24 in trouble. "He looks like he's on fire!"

The burning bomber continued on course for home. Like a gut-shot dog caught killing sheep, this one followed its instincts, as though somehow everything would be all right if it could just make it home. But the black trail that stained the sky behind it testified to the guilty one as sure as a blood trail in the snow. For seven minutes the cripple clung to the home trail, dropping lower and lower as the pain of its injuries slowed it down. Then it blew all to hell. . . .

Four parachutes were counted. Four out of ten. . . .

As we approached the Belgian coast on the way out, something mysterious was happening. In the approaching darkness, we could easily see flashes from the ground batteries. But, there were no telltale black bursts to mark the aerial explosions. As we headed out over the water, another bomber flamed down from a group behind us.

On order from the group lead, we split up in three-ship elements when we were well over the North Sea. England was in total darkness as we approached except for an occasional light flickering here and there for the benefit of approaching bomber groups. Finally the darkness swept up to envelop our little formations, and we turned on our navigational lights. As we came in over land, search lights came up and converged over the various airfields, in cones of brightness. There was one unusually large, red ground flare. Then, Rowland cut in on interphone.

"Turn out the lights. Just got the order. Enemy planes have followed us back!"

Now I knew what the big red ground *flare* was that I had just seen and wondered about. The Luftwaffe was on our tail finding easy pickings. I turned off everything but our wing tip lights. My element lead started to circle a convergence of beacons over the wrong field. After several circles, while I listened in on landing instructions, I realized he was trying to get instructions from our base to land on the wrong airport. I called him and gently suggested that we get home. He was just as confident that he was right. After another try couldn't shake him, I swung away and dropped in over the 44th. We wanted to get down. Later reports indicated that Jerry caught ten bombers before they landed, and the British ack-ack, improperly informed about our late mission, had also knocked down a number of American planes before the word got around.

We finally received permission to land. It was an eerie feeling when we eased onto the runway. All the gunners strained for sight of enemy planes with the prayer that none would come blazing out of the darkness when we were in our most vulnerable position.

Taxiing with lights off, I tried to follow the tiny beams that marked the edge of the taxi strip on each side of the jeep leading us to the dispersal area. The ground crew, for whom this was also a "first," was having its troubles. Our jeep took us past our parking area. When an empty one showed up, I pulled in to make a turn around so that I could get back where I belonged. A GI with a flashlight was doing his best to guide me around, but suddenly our bomber lurched and came to a stop.

Our right wheel had run off the edge of the hardtop and was sunk in three feet of soft earth. The mission was over. Seven hours. Six hours of daytime flying and another lifetime packed into the other sixty minutes of night flying.

Before transportation to the briefing room arrived, two trucks moved in and attached to our stranded bomber with heavy cables. They had the plane back on he macadam before we climbed into the truck sent for us.

At the debriefing, *I* was the one surprised when S-2 expressed no astonishment over Renfro's report on the red airplane. "We've been getting some reports on new jet airplanes that the Germans are building," Intelligence told me. "We're interested in anything like this that we can get. We don't know too much yet about it."

Two thirds of a bottle of Scotch was always available at these sessions for each crew. Since several of my boys didn't drink at all, and none of us felt much like it with our nasal passages already dried out from being on oxygen for prolonged periods, we had been leaving a considerable amount in the bottle. Then, a letter from my brother Wayne, who was with an artillery unit at Southhampton waiting for invasion of the continent, gave me an inspiration. I began to take our leavings back to the barracks and add each to the little nest egg being accumulated for a reunion with him. A meeting was in the making—contingent, of course, upon my being able to wrangle a leave for London. As of the moment, things didn't look favorable, but the barracks bottle was building up some pleasant prospects.

This evening, my officers and I wandered over to the officers' club where a dance had been scheduled. A contingent of girls from Norwich was to have been brought to the base to assuage the loneliness of the officers and to provide dancing partners. Only the debris of the night's entertainment greeted us. Not only were the girls gone (S-2 kept us too long), but the ground-pounders had consumed all the liquor.

The combination of circumstances, surrounding the dance and the late mission, gave us all cause to ponder. It is unlikely that our conclusions were in accordance with all the facts in the case.

Whatever the circumstances, the late mission had one good aftermath. No mission was scheduled on the bulletin board. It looked like a real, restful Sunday was in the making.

But Mars was smiling a crooked smile. Wars are like that.

11

These are true heroes, these the men,
Though living now, or honored dead,
Who wear the crown upon their head
Of nobler life or rich amen.
                    From "About Bravery"

Sunday, April 23, 1944, a day of rest.

We needed it. It was always figured that an hour of flying while in training was equal to two hours of any other kind of work. I wouldn't attempt to equate an hour of combat with any other type of effort. All I knew was that, from the moment the throttles were eased forward on all four engines for takeoff, something opened the drain on every corpuscle and every brain cell. When the switches were cut on the hard stand, whether it was three hours or eight hours later, our well-conditioned brains and bodies had been reduced to a soggy mass of gray matter and meat.

The debriefing officers from S-2 were masters at wringing out what was left to get whatever information we could remember or produce from the navigator's log. They were patient fellows who never made light of anything they could drag from the fog of our thinking. They had a gentle touch with words, a sympathetic rapport, like a mother trying to get the true story from a child who has been badly bruised and can't quite understand why.

After twenty-nine hours and fifteen minutes in the air of the past one hundred, there wasn't much left. I wandered over to the hut to talk to my noncoms, the kids who had been shoved into manhood over a period of just two weeks. They looked like men—like tired, drawn men with pale, pinched faces. Their grins when they saw me were genuine, but they lacked luster. Something wrenched inside me when I looked at their faces that such a short time ago had radiated the eagerness and the energy that knowledge and confidence in their several duties had instilled in them. The knowledge was still there, and the skill, but the confidence had been sucked from them. You can't build confidence on a bombing mission. You can't direct your energy to seek out the enemy and destroy him or be destroyed in a rip-roaring sky battle. You just sit and sweat and be alert to defend yourself if the enemy seeks you out, and you drop bombs when the signal is given. And your bombs drop down toward a point that might be a target or a hospital or a rabbit in a patch of woods.

"Enjoying your vacation, Lieutenant?"

Bill Sanders grinned up from the letter he was writing. The third pair of eyes on the flight deck, my engineer shared whatever torture was imposed upon Jack and me as he stood between us on takeoff. He sweated out every miss in an engine, every needle that trembled between normal and the redline, the whine and wheeze of the landing gear and the flaps, uncertainty of the gasoline supply. For, if anything went wrong with the airplane, it was Sanders to whom I must turn. He was quietly proud of his job, and I was proud to have him as my engineer. After takeoff, when he climbed into his top turret, it was comforting to have him near at hand.

I still didn't know much about any of them except for the time we had shared together since we had been assigned to each other. Longest with me was the bombardier, Jay L. Davis, who had introduced himself back at

Salt Lake City as Larry. He and I were the nucleus of the crew.

Then we picked up a co-pilot who was only with us long enough to get over being mad at the B-24 after coming to us qualified as a first pilot on the B-17. He was another victim of the hurry to develop pilots faster than airplanes were coming off the assembly lines. Some of his antagonism splashed off on me. There were quite a number in the same situation, and it took time for them to adjust to the unhappy fact that they were now co-pilots. About the time that all of them became resigned to their fate, and each team of pilots was pulling together in the traces, in came a group fresh out of twin-engine advanced school! With only days remaining, we lost our well-oriented co-pilots. Mine was given a crew of his own, and he went on to die somewhere in his part of the war.

It was quite a jolt. It was the day before Christmas that the experienced co-pilots were taken from us—with nine weeks remaining before we would take off for Europe. My Christmas present had been the big, good-natured package from the West Coast.

Jack Emerson caught on quickly with the rest of the crew although his annoying casualness had at first been a source of personal concern. It did not interfere with the skills he brought with his twenty years of life, but he had a lot of catching up to do. It was December 28 when he first donned an oxygen mask. It was January 30 before I had a chance to give him his first landing with a B-24. We were still practicing landings for him on the way over via Brazil and Africa!

Dale Rauscher was an erstwhile pilot who had to turn his talents to navigating when his training plane and he failed to come to terms fast enough to please the Army. At twenty seven, he was the old man of the crew, who shipped in with his wife on December 27 to Casper, Wyoming, to complete the crew.

The rest of the crew had been around a bit longer. Leonard Rowland, who sweated out a transfer from our crew to pilot training until the powers-that-be decided we needed him more than they did, was a product of Oregon. For our money he was one of the best things to come out of the Northwest.

He had come in with Sanders, who hailed from Illinois, and George Cox, armorer, from the hills of West Virginia, at Salt Lake City a long time before, so it now seemed, on November 1. Ten days later, Harry Schow, a married sergeant from Chicago, who had also tried pilot training; Walter Reichert, from Illinois; and the pride of Texas, George Renfro, filled out the gunnery manpower.

As Sanders greeted me with that grin and his, "Enjoying your vacation, Lieutenant?" something deep inside of me glowed with a warmth not altogether consistent with proper military attitude. I didn't see much of these young men, even on the airplane. But I felt their presence and sensed their dedication amid the garble of light and serious talk over the interphone. These were *my* men. In the informal atmosphere of their quarters where I was the welcomed intruder, I felt a great affection, a great dependent affection for them. My very life depended upon *them*.

The talk was light. We didn't discuss the number of missions left, a sordid subject, but the weather took the usual mauling. They had each either been writing or reading letters from home, and I didn't stay. The many unspoken words had been said, and my visit provided the exchange we needed. I tried not to think of the things that could happen to any one or all of these young men who counted on me to bring them back each time. I was counting on them to make it possible.

The first inkling that our day of rest might be disturbed came as I was rattling out a letter that evening to Eloise on the typewriter I had nurtured from the States. Jack passed a remark, intended to be casual.

"I don't feel so good in the stomach." Then he tried to pass it off. "Just a little bellyache; must have eaten too much."

"You'd better report to the hospital and get something for it," I suggested.

"No, I'll be okay."

I insisted. "We're up for the mission tomorrow. I don't want to get stuck with another co-pilot. Take off!"

Jack groaned his reluctance for a few minutes, but then he disappeared in the direction of the hospital. I continued my one-sided conversation with my wife. By the time I hit the usual, but so necessary, sentiment on the last line, I was feeling a bit uncomfortable where *my* dinner sat. Maybe it was the glue on the back of the envelope that touched off my trouble. But within seconds I was on the way to the john, running.

I just got my head inside the door when everything in my guts gave way. It was what the nurse who was my wife would have called a projectile emesis. I simply blew. Everything that wasn't tied down came bursting out in one big blast that sprayed the inside of the small building. There were a few afterbursts, then it was over. So I thought.

Someone came by and offered to call the ambulance. I declined.

"No, I feel fine now. Guess I got rid of what ailed me." And I meant it, every stupid word of it.

Five minutes later I was lying in a ditch at the ambulance stop with both hands clutching at the pain in my insides. My first blast had been a good one, there was nothing left to throw up. Yet my wretching stomach continued its efforts to expel what wasn't there. Within minutes that took hours, the ambulance pulled up, and I feebly climbed aboard.

If I hadn't been ill, a few seconds in the meat wagon would have put me in sick bay. The inside reeked with vomit that was slippery underfoot, and the benches were crowded with men retching until all that was left was their own blood, and that come up. When we reached the base hospital, all the beds were taken. Harried medics directed me to a stretcher on the floor between two cots. There I groveled until a white uniform knelt by my head.

"Is there anything I can do that you think might help?"

I asked for water, "so I'll have something to throw up."

At least the water lubricated my fiery throat as it went down—and promptly came back up, still cold. Finally, somebody slipped a shot of morphine into my arm, and I stumbled through a mental fog until a blessed numbness took over my pain. But chills and fever alternated throughout the night long after morphine had quieted down the hospital enough for those lucky ones who could sleep.

Toward morning, sleep came to me. It was nearly noon before I woke up to find that I was in a cot and the hospital was almost cleared of the mob scene of the night before. They turned me loose, and I made my shaky way back to the hut. Jack was in good shape.

"There were about a hundred and forty hit by the food poisoning," he said. "The medics think it was the Boston cream pie. Some of the ingredients were spoiled." Then he grinned and mentioned the name of a chicken-shit major. "At least something good came out of it. He had several pieces of pie, and it really knocked him. He's still in the hospital."

I shared Jack's pleasure. No one could satisfactorily explain why the rank of major seemed to settle upon every crummy bastard in the Army. There were fine majors, especially among the flying officers, but the paddlefeet with the gold oak leaf seemed to fit into a class all their own. Some said it was because they were bucking for lieutenant colonel. But *everybody* wanted to move up a rank. Majors must have wanted to more than anyone else.

Like the one who came tearing down the taxi strip at Dakar, French West Africa, right on the edge of the lion country. Apparently he had picked me up through a binocular while I was shooting craps with the enlisted men. His jeep threw up a cloud of the red dust that covered everything and he hit the strip on the run.

"Lieutenant, were you gambling with your enlisted men?"

The two dimes in the dust didn't leave much room for quibbling.

"Yes sir. We have two hours to kill while the mechanics

check out an engine that burned too much gas coming across from Brazil. Just something to do," I added lamely.

The good major then proceeded to dress me down with remarks generally reserved for criminal rape cases or triple homicide—all this in front of my enlisted men—strictly verboten in good Army circles. After all this, he included a few choice penalties to be imposed if he should "ever catch" me again, despite the fact that we were scheduled to head north 1,700 miles to Marraketch in a couple hours.

Consequently, I was delighted to learn that the meathead who made a hog of himself on the Boston cream pie had really been creamed by the bugs. My delight was short-lived. I was unable to keep anything on *my* stomach and they sent me back to the hospital for another night. This time I really enjoyed my stay and got some needed rest. I wasn't sick, but the medics were trying to beef up my innards so that they would accept food again.

I didn't miss anything. There were so many flying officers laid up that missions were scrubbed for the two days. Fortunately, there were no serious aftereffects. All of us could speculate on whether something really went sour at the cookhouse or one of Hitler's emissaries slipped a pill in our pudding.

12

I've known above warmth from your sunny smiles
While frowned you coldly on those all below
With glances stretching out for endless miles—
From "Oh Clouds; My Clouds"

We needed another easy one to rejuvenate our confidence and chalk up another mission on the tally to our ticket home. Gutersloh provided it. Actually, the target was another airport near this city something over 250 miles airline from where we assembled in the middle of the night for briefing. The 44th had failed to knock out the airfield on the last try, and we were being given a second chance. After three days of *rest*, occasioned by the hospital exercise, headquarters apparently thought we would welcome a ride to Germany. Whatever the reasoning, we were roused from our sacks at 1:15 A.M. to make ready.

It was another takeoff in complete darkness with only the blinking signal from the tail of the ship ahead to guide us to assembly. An overcast stomped down the darkness, but the air was smooth and uncluttered to 6,000 feet.

Then we broke through the cloud cover in a crescendo of color to meet the rising sun. Ahead, one continuous flock of misty sheep crowded crimson back to crimson back in unending pasture that hid the ugly war from view. There were only the proud Liberators cutting through the color to mar the scene. Yet the graceful Libs had a beauty of their own which belied their tragic intent as they lifted in unison above the carpet of clouds that gradually paled to white as the sun confidently raced us toward the heavens.

The formation was snug but not the white-knuckled tightness we had known on most of our trips. I was actually enjoying the ride. Except for the 500-pounders clustered in our bomb racks, this trip was not unlike some of the hops we had made coming over from the States.

Jack was flying her now, and he was committed, for better or for worse, to finish the tour as our co-pilot. The day before, when we had a chance to relax between the hospital and this trip, I had a chance to make good on my promise to recommend him for his own crew. Doing so wasn't easy. He was a good man to have in the right seat. And, I dreaded the chore of working in a new pilot. Maybe it was because we were still a lonely entity, still a replacement crew, and we still did not feel quite as though we were a real part of the group. The move from the 66th to the 67th Squadron had thrown us in with a new cadre of officers before we had a chance to know even the names of all of the old ones. Maybe this was why Jack had his answer when I braced him back in the barracks.

"Look, Jackson." I limped my way into the subject. "First I want you to know that I'm perfectly satisfied with your flying. That's why I want to talk to you about it." John F. Emerson gave me a half-embarrassed grin and waited me out. He was reading me. "You know that I promised I would recommend you for your own crew as soon as I felt you were ready." I took a deep breath and let it out. "You're ready."

Jack clamped his hands about one knee and rocked back a moment before answering. He didn't hesitate long.

"I've thought about it," he said. "And I've decided I would rather finish this tour with the crew."

We sat there for a brief time in an uneasy silence. I didn't question then, or ever, the reasons for his decision. But whatever they might have been, to me it was the high point in my time with the military. He hadn't even said that he wanted to finish with *me*. It was enough that he wanted to continue as a part of the crew. The rest of the crew was bound to me through their complete dependence upon my flying ability, or lack of it, although I was certain that a real bond of affection existed among all the members. We had no serious problems. But a co-pilot had an incipient independence that at any time might override whatever allegiance or affection he might feel for a crew. Although the title, Airplane Commander, was rather an ethereal one, it was nevertheless the goal of every bomber pilot at some time in his career. Jack had chosen to relinquish whatever rights or desires he might have had at that moment to continue with us. I was mightily pleased.

"I'm sure you know we'll be damned glad to have you."

And now, as I looked over at the tall kid from California, I *was* damned glad to have him. I would have special reasons to be glad before many more hours had passed under our wings.

On the same day that Jack and I discussed his immediate future as a pilot, I had another discussion at squadron headquarters. With six missions, two recalls, and an abortion for a total of just short of fifty combat hours, I felt the crew was being neglected in the promotion department. I was particularly concerned for the non-coms. Another stripe meant a lot to them.

"We know that many of the crews received promotions before leaving the States. And, we were assured that, after five missions, promotions would be automatic. I've got a damned fine crew, and I feel that they deserve consideration. We've got six in, and we're up for tomorrow."

The operations officer seemed surprised that no one had caught the "oversight." He checked our record more closely.

"I see," he finally said, looking up. "You came over here from the 66th Squadron, and your name was placed on the bottom of the list." He shuffled some more papers. "Yes, I see your name is on the bottom of the list for leaves, too."

I groaned. "If they keep moving us around, we never will get anywhere."

He returned my half grin. It wasn't all kidding, and he knew it. "I'll check this out for you," he promised. "You'll hear from us."

But now we were busy with the seventh mission on our second try to Gutersloh. Flak was beginning to reach up through the overcast. This was the primary consideration in determining whether or not a flight toward combat would be considered a full-blown mission. If your plane was fired upon by flak or fighters, it was a mission regardless of whether or not you turned back after the action. On the other hand, a pilot forced to abort from deep within enemy territory would likely be credited with a mission whether or not he saw enemy action from the ground or the air. Providing, of course, that he had a legitimate reason for aborting.

Despite the flak, this one was a real milk run. No sweat. The flak was heavy in spots, but none of it came anywhere near the formation. And then friendly fighters moved in overhead to further cement our feelings of comparative security. It was always a nervous wait when fighters were first sighted until they came close enough for identification. However, if the German fighters came first, appearance of our fighter formations was akin to finding a shed during a downpour on a long hike from home. Our little friends couldn't stay long, particularly when we were well inside Germany, but they were most welcome to stay as long as their gas supply would permit.

We were right on our E.T.A. at the target. The lead navigator did a top job in taking us to the drop area. Not one airplane had been damaged; not one had been forced to abort. It was a perfect mission to that point. There the planning, the preparation, the execution of the mission broke down. We couldn't drop!

Jack switched to interphone. "We're going home. We can't drop through these clouds." Even as he spoke, the lead box began a slow sweep to head for home. The trip back was as uneventful as the ride to the target. One by one we dipped to the runway with our load of 500-pounders. Even as we trucked our way back to headquarters, the incongruity of the easy one, despite our pleasure at being back without pain, stood almost stark against our experience to the moment.

It had been five hours and thirty minutes from takeoff to landing. This, too, was a mission. And the bulletin board said we would have another tomorrow.

13

Or some drop deep in Neptune's nest
To feel his mighty fingers mesh
And crush the spirit from their breast
While fish find feed on worthless flesh.
From "A Pilot's Plea"

April 27, 1944.

This was to be the longest day. Mars had a special plan for us, and those to whom we turned for orders compounded the special agony reserved for our replacement crew on April 27, 1944. April 8, the day of our first mission, seemed more like nineteen months into history than the actual nineteen days of our little war. And the pleasant respite provided by the easy one of the twenty-sixth largely dissolved into grumbles as we were awakened at 2:15 A.M.

We climbed mechanically into our flying clothes, trying to cling to some part of our interrupted sleep. But as always, consciousness won out, albeit more slowly than usual, and we staggered to briefing. It was obvious by the confusion that somebody had crossed their wires. Takeoff was scheduled for 7:30 A.M.!

By now everybody was completely awake and briefing-room confusion gradually evolved into the usual pattern of Mae West rows as " 'Tenshun!'' brought us to our feet for the colonel's grand entrance. Spirits were somewhat restored as the trip was outlined. It looked like a made-to-order mission.

"This should be a real easy one," we were told. "You will go right in and right out. We are after rocket installations near Montivilliers in France. All of your flying will be over water except for your bombing run. You'll be carrying eight 1,000-pounders, and you'll drop in train at two-second intervals."

While the briefing officer was at work, we could hear the increasing drone of airplanes overhead. However, we had heard no alert and paid them no attention. It could be British coming back or weather ships checking things out upstairs.

Suddenly there was a twin explosion as Jerry dropped a couple eggs in the barracks area. We learned later that the bombs had merely torn up a section of sod and tossed a few splinters through one of the barracks. The briefing officer hesitated only a second, grinned, and went on with his work.

"One thing we want to emphasize. Although you will only be over the coast a very short time, there are some heavy flak guns around those rocket ramps. As soon as you get your bombs away, make a sharp turn right and get the hell out of there. Those kids are good!"

Several times during the briefing he re-emphasized the need to turn away quickly after the drop. But the prospects of getting in a quick one dispelled any apprehension about the flak guns. Everybody was in good spirits and we killed time while waiting around for takeoff.

We had a bit of the new and the old for this one. Our squadrons would be split into javelins, three-ship elements in line, so that the bomb pattern would be confined to an area no wider than three bombers in formation. It was a probe for the heavily camouflaged V-1 installations, soon to be pounding southern England. It required no special flying know-how, but it would be the first that our plane was scheduled for such a formation. On the old side was the *Wasp Nest*, dirty and feeble, squatting in her dispersal area with twenty-four missions behind her without an abortion. The crew chief was especially solicitous toward me as he guaranteed that everything was shipshape. I knew that he had probably given his personal attention to every rivet and nut before we appeared. If we got her out and could bring her back, he would earn his Soldier's Medal. Still, she was the *Wasp Nest*, and there was only so much you could do for her any more. I was glad it was a short one.

We wheezed into position, and I called on every wasp as we trundled down the strip with a bellyful of trouble. She made it with room to spare, but the old *Nest* was sluggish and I had to push her with everything she had. Nevertheless, she slid into her assigned slot, however reluctantly, and we were on our way. It should have been that way to landing, for we came in over the French coast in tight formation and swung south for the rockets.

On signal, the bombs began to drip like blobs from a leaky oil valve. Each release gave an almost imperceptible lift to the tired bomber until all eight were gone and I had Larry's "Bombs away!" The rumble and final thump of the bomb doors should have been the signal for our turn. All airplanes had dropped on the lead bomber's release.

But we didn't turn; and we didn't turn! The briefing officer's warning kept running through my mind: "Get the hell out of there; get the hell out of there; get the hell out of there!" I found myself screaming into my oxygen mask. "Turn, you son of a bitch! Turn, you bastard! Turn! Turn! Turn!" What in the *hell* was he waiting for?

We hadn't had a piece of flak. I was straining to keep from peeling away from my element. The mission was over. Still we continued in a straight line, the same heading on which we had bombed. Then it came.

At first the flak was off to our left, big black mushrooms that indicated at least 128-mm guns. At the first burst, our head ship finally began to bank to the right. But it was too late. By the time the movement had been relayed to me and I whipped along behind the spear of bombers, the ground gunners had us bracketed. The big bursts were right among us. And, they followed us even as we crossed the coast. Then we were almost out of it.

Maybe it was a desperation try, because the flak was drifting toward the rear of the formation. Maybe it was the last volley of four. But—*it was there!*

Even as I watched the element lead directly ahead of me, instinctively holding close formation although our bombs were long gone, minutes behind us, it happened! He caught a direct hit just starboard of the number three engine. The wing flapped up as though on a hinge, and the hinge was a bolt of orange-red flame and black smoke. The extra lift of the good wing threw the bomber into a right snap roll before the pilot had a chance to catch it. And from the moving picture screen of my windshield, the Liberator twisted down out of sight. Instinctively I ducked aside as debris from the doomed one crashed into my center windshield and shattered the bulletproof glass.

"He's spinning, still spinning," I heard as from a distance over my interphones. The airplane was as good as dead, and now it had no personality. My crewmen spoke of her pilot. Now it was "he" spinning. And *he* was a crew of ten men whirling like the burning winglet of a maple seed. Human flesh was being smashed by centrifugal force against the metal guts of the dying one as her crew tried to scramble for the exits. Then came the inevitable "There she goes; blew all to hell!" Use of "she" exonerated the pilot of any part of this sordid happening as again, in this desperate instant when she gave up in a ball of flame, the Liberator had her last identity. We were well out over the water when it happened, and any who got out would . . . my thought were cut off by the interphone: "No chutes."

Ahead, the wingmen of the fallen bomber held their positions. There was only a piece of empty sky ahead of and between them where moments before the leader of their element had marked trail for us. I couldn't stand that empty sky, and I forced the reluctant *Wasp Nest* into the blank hole. Still the question burned into my brain, "Why didn't he turn?" It came out later that the lead ship wanted to get good pictures of the bomb drop. I hope the pictures were good.

The kid who went down was on his 24th.

The crew chief waved us into position at the dispersal area with jumbled emotions. He could count. But the one missing plane could not completely conceal his pleasure of getting back the old *Wasp Nest*. He could have her now. I marked up two of the engines for replacement and ran smack into an argument with the engineer who met me on the hard stand. He didn't go along with my contention that the *Nest* was no longer fit to fly without a complete going over.

"I won't take her up again," I informed him. I meant it. His "We'll see" did no more than make me burn. But this one thing they hadn't taken from the meager authority permitted the so-called airplane commander. I didn't have to fly any airplane I didn't think was reasonably airworthy—as long as I had damned good reasons and could back them up.

I felt my reasons were strong enough when the squadron CO met me moments later. When his jeep swirled to a screeching halt at the edge of the dispersal area where we awaited transportation, I knew something was up.

"Think you can stand another one today?" he grinned.

I allowed as how I could, but ". . . not in this one. She's had it." I told him of my writeup on the bomber. "She's had all she can take without a couple new engines." The CO said nothing on this score. However, he did fill me in briefly on the afternoon trip.

"It shouldn't be a bad one. You might get some flak, but it won't be a long hop."

We barely had time to finish our lunch before the loud-speaker at the dining room blared out, "All pilots report to the briefing room immediately." The group that filed into the room a short time later was anything but eager. It was near noon, and we had been on our eyes for nearly ten hours. No mission for us could be an easy one now. However, it didn't look too bad as the briefing officer hurried through instructions. Something over three hundred miles one way, our penetration would be about 150 miles inland to the railway yards at Chalons Sur Marne. Since we were cutting south for a northern bomb run, we would be able to see Paris for the first time through our right windows—if the weather held. This brought a laugh and eased the tension further. But, we all tightened up with the next announcement.

"You will be bombing from 14,000 feet."

The groan that went up was genuine. Many of us had never bombed at less than 18,000, usually at 20,000, and higher. This would be like dragging our trailing antenna on the roof tops. However, the briefing officer emphasized the importance of smashing the railroad yards. "Our information indicates that there is a heavy concentration of rolling stock there today." It was another job to do. We were given a good course which should take us around all flak concentrations. Before we broke up for separate briefings, the group CO took over.

"You will be making history today," he informed us. "This will be the first time ever that heavy bombers have attempted two missions in the same day. I know you are tired, and we are sorry about getting you up so early this morning before the mission, but this shouldn't be too tough."

His words were sincere, but they could not erase the uncomfortable feeling that we were not fully ready for this trip. Always before, no matter how early or how late we started, we had a reserve of freshness ready as soon as we shook the sleepwebs of early morning or gathered our resources for the big effort later in the day. We were already tired, and we were just starting this mission.

However, any personal lassitude disappeared when I was given my ship assignment. It was one of the same model as long-gone *Sweet Eloise*. A Lieutenant Steinke had flown her over via the southern route, and I knew him to be an excellent pilot. This was the one time I was really anxious to get to the flight line.

Despite the heavy lunch and the warm spring sun, I was no longer sleepy.

14

Faith, to sustain, must have been strong
And deep enough before his fight,
To question not if this be wrong,
But know, by God, his end is right.
                    From "Faith"

Grins on the faces of Bill Sanders—especially Sanders, Emerson, and Rowland reflected the sentiments of all of us as I climbed into the nearly new airplane. The engineer was bubbling over.

"She checks out great!" he said as I slid into the high-backed seat. "This one is just like the one we brought over."

"I only hope we can keep her," I tossed back at Sanders, and Jack supported the hope.

"It's quite a difference after the junk we've been flying."

I plugged in my electrical suit connection and checked the oxygen mask. The seat adjusted firmly into place, full forward as usual. Everything was crisp and new. Even the paint on the throttle quadrant was unchecked. Behind the levity of the moment was a tentative confidence that maybe this airplane was a fast step upward in the slow progress we had been making in our effort to become a more integral part of the 44th Bomb Group. I felt somehow that we could do a real job with this beauty without the nagging fear that a bad engine or sick supercharger would make every mission a major journey of fear before we had even crossed the North Sea. The plane didn't even have a name yet, she was that new.

It was getting warm behind the windshield. I slid my side window back for air as the squadron CO slipped under the left wing in his jeep.

"What do you think of her?" he questioned, his expression obviously receptive for the expected answer.

"She's beautiful," I called back with undisguised enthusiasm. "At last we have an *airplane.*" I hesitated, then tried him with the question on the minds of the entire crew. "If we take care of her, can we have her?"

His grin softened, an almost imperceptible acknowledgment of the seriousness behind my little trial balloon. "I'll see what I can do, Schuyler." The tone of his voice indicated that he understood, and that he would try to have the B-24 assigned to us permanently. Maybe he understood much more than I had suspected. Because, as though suddenly conscious of our somewhat frustrating journey to this moment, he became conversational about the mission.

"Don't let this one bother you, Schuyler. It really shouldn't be a bad one. It may be a little rough over the target area, but we've laid out a course that should keep you out of trouble going in and coming out." His grin came back. "You're making history. Good luck!" He waved and nodded to his driver, then zoomed around the front of the Liberator to spread more cheer down the line. He left me with a good feeling inside as though, for the first time, someone really recognized that we *were* a part of the 44th; and more importantly, that someone cared.

At age twenty-four, you are instinctively looking for *some* kind of recognition. Especially, if you are a bomber pilot and you have sweated through the strain and hazards of learning to be a bomber pilot and an airplane commander, you are looking for some nod from somebody who recognizes that you are around. As an aviation cadet, you are daily impressed with the fact that there is nothing lower in the army than you. Even the lowest private has more status until you wash out and become a private yourself or reach the doubtful day when they award you wings. You cannot help but think back to happenings which were routine in training. They would make headlines in peace times, but they were common in the rush to make fighting men out of kids who weren't mad at anybody. Like that time back at Casper, Wyoming.

On a routine practice mission, you are coming back to base, and you lower your gear routinely. Only, the nose wheel won't straighten up. It is cocked at a 45° angle. A normal landing with the nose wheel in this position would slam it back through the airplane like a projectile, and somebody, maybe everybody, would be killed. So you call in for an emergency landing. And, you tell the crew members to cushion themselves against the bulkheads with parachutes and anything else they can find handy so that they might live through the crash if your landing isn't perfect. Or even if it is perfect. Then, as you are in the landing pattern, preparing to make that one try to get the crew and the B-24 on the ground safely, the field commander comes on the radio.

"Pull her up for a few minutes, Lieutenant, I want to talk to you," he says.

You bank away from the field which has already been cleared for you. As you drop a wing, you can't help but notice the fire trucks and ambulances gathered at the end of the runway and the growing crowd of GI's lining the edge to see what happens when a Liberator comes in with the nose wheel cocked. While you are pulling away, you have a chance to glance at Sergeant Sanders and Lieutenant Emerson. Their faces are pale and drawn, like you feel deep inside where your guts are knotted into a tight, nerve-wrapped ball.

Word from the tower has only given temporary relief. You already had your plans made for the landing. Touch her down softly, nose high; hold her back on the skid, shut off the engines and every electrical switch to minimize the chance of fire if that nose wheel comes slamming back through the airplane. And you can't touch the brakes, for this would throw the weight forward. But you listen to the colonel.

"Whatever you do, don't touch the brakes," he says. "Have the men cushion themselves against the bulkheads. Turn off the engines as soon as you are on the runway." You "Yes sir" the colonel to acknowledge each suggestion, taking inner satisfaction in the fact that you have anticipated each although there are no tech orders to cover such an emergency. "Have several of the men go clear to the tail of the plane to help hold it down." There is one you didn't think of. You send three of the gunners to the tail. "Okay, Schuyler, you are on your own."

Then, once again you swing in toward the field, taking a glimmer of satisfaction in the fact that you don't have to follow the usual flight pattern. The field is still closed to all traffic and will be until you are down. The hedgerow crowd along the runway is growing as the word spreads. You throttle back and drop your flaps for a normal approach. The wind is light, and you can keep the wings level as you shoot for the near edge of the runway. You need all the runway you can get without brakes. You ease her onto the concrete, tail low, and the sudden drag of rubber makes her pitch a little—a little pitch that forces your heart toward your throat. But at one hundred miles per hour, you still have control, and you ease the tail back down. Then you are rolling, you are on the runway. You switch off all four engines. Instinctively your toes want to test the brakes on top of the rudder pedals, but you hold them back, feeling with the elevators to get the skid against the concrete. You feel it—and hear it. The metallic drag will help slow you if you don't pull back too hard and break the skid or rub it off on the concrete. You can sense the shower of sparks that must be trailing the tail.

With deliberate speed, Jack is turning off all auxiliary switches. The tail begins to lighten, and you are losing your elevators as the plane slows down. Then, ponderously, the great nose eases forward as you uselessly bury the wheel in your stomach. The nose wheel catches, there is a great sideways lurch, the plane straightens . . . you are rolling straight. Slowly you trundle to a stop, trust yourself to look at Jack and Bill, share a sigh of relief. There is a tow vehicle speeding across the runway toward your ship.

While they are hooking up the tow bar, you see another vehicle coming. It is a jeep, and the base CO swings in below your window.

"Everything all right?" he asks. You nod. "Nice work, Schuyler," he says. And this is enough. Three words are sufficient compensation for everything you have put into your job, the months of trying.

But when you came back on that night flight to Amarillo, Texas, with gasoline streaming from a defective cap right over a supercharger that usually, and did this time, flame on landing, you merely broke up another card game at the firehouse. It was the middle of the night. You anticipated the defective supercharger and blew it out with a blast of the throttle when it flamed. All they did was to replace the defective cap and send you on for your trip from Casper to Amarillo and back, nonstop, that night.

Nobody said anything when you took off on three engines that day at Casper when number three ran away after you had reached the point of no return down the runway. With only three engines, you had to buck the downdrafts from 8,000-foot Casper Range and get enough altitude to bring the sick bomber around for a landing. It was no comfort when engineering informed you, as they had with the bad shimmy dampener on the nose wheel, that they had had previous trouble with the prop governor on that airplane.

You just thanked God at the end of each day, or whenever you could find the time, that you were alive. And you wondered what happened one night a short time later when *Tantalizing Tillie* didn't make it and blew up in a ball of flame and flesh off the end of that same runway. You cursed maintenance and you cursed engineering with no more than passing knowledge of what their problems were with the beat-up bombers sent back from the war in Europe.

Then there was that other day on an air to ground sim-
ulated strafing mission when number three started to die
as you were dragging the sand at full throttle toward a
pass between the rugged peaks. . . .

But it was not the trouble, the threats to life and limb,
the cold nights that you flew without heaters, the pace that
bothered you. Other crews were going through some of
the same or worse. It was simply that you wanted, after
all this, to belong somewhere. You wanted to be a part of
this goddamned war!

And, now, on this April 27, as the flare to start engines
rocketed above the field for the mission to Chalons sur
Marne, I suddenly felt a part of the 67th Bomb Squadron,
44th Bomb Group, 14th Combat Wing, 66th Bomb De-
tachment, 8th Air Force. We belonged!

As I bent the throttles toward the instrument panel, our
bomb-laden bird shuddered and shook against the brakes,
quivering like a setter on leash the first morning of the
hunting season. She *wanted* to fly. When I kicked the
brakes loose, she hurried down the runway with a feel of
power that vibrated away the misgivings and fears that had
begun to plague us.

The sun was high and bright. But it was well off to our
right as we climbed into the blue above the southeast horizon on the North Sea. Moving into our position on the
left wing of the lead in the second section was no problem.
It was comforting to be out of the coffin corner at the rear
in a ship that could carry its own weight and a load of
bombs with ease. We were moving up.

15

But some took the count, and blood failed to quell
Fire that flared through warm flesh and cold steel,
and some dropped black buds that bloomed as they fell,
Crumbs from the table of Mars' mid-day meal.
                    From "First Time To The Target"

We headed down over the English Channel after assembling on course. The lead ship climbed slowly, and we had only 15,000 feet when we approached the French coast on a course which would take us somewhat south of the target. This would keep the Krauts guessing and permit us to bomb on a northerly course. After bombs were away, we could simply swing on a course to the northwest and home.

Flak at the coast was moderate. It didn't damage anything more than our nerves because of the relatively low altitude, and the entire group drifted safely through. We had come to have a healthy respect for the ground guns, but somehow the black blobs held less terror than usual. I felt some of the old confidence that came to me that day back in Tennessee when my love affair with the Liberator came into full being. This one answered to the controls like a good cow pony that senses your intentions before it feels the touch of the rein on its neck. I turned her over to Jack. It was only moments until his eyes transmitted his grin of satisfaction at the response to the controls.

As we approached the Paris area, flak suddenly began to bloom in earnest. The lead box started violent evasive action. Weaving in and out of the more obvious concentrations, the formation started to splinter as all of us were hard put to hold position. Then the upper air cleared, and the 44th melted back into three solid swarms. Jack jerked his thumb ahead to the right for my attention.

Dimly, through a ground haze which reflected the lowering sun, we saw Paris. "Take a good look," I suggested over the interphone. "This may be as close as any of you will ever get to Paris." I ignored the suggestions that came flooding back about landing, "just for the night."

Soon the formation turned abruptly north. It was not difficult to find the target area. Already it was being pounded by other formations. And they were being pasted in turn by fighters. In rapid succession Renfro called out kills.

"Fighter going down about ten o'clock. Too far away to tell if it is ours. There goes another one . . . two of them!"

Friendly fighters had engaged Germans pecking at the lumbering B-17's which had first crack at the target. We were dropping down to bombing altitude, preparing to follow several other B-24 groups that were moving in. Then one, and yet another B-17 dropped below their formations. Like bits of debris floating on water, they had held position until they absorbed too much and started undulating down, down, smoking . . . smoking badly, the flame hardly visible from the distance . . . then a great, grisly rose of black and red as the only visible tribute to their dying.

Directly ahead, the preceding B-24's were unloading, adding their bit of hell to the churning maelstrom of smoke and fire in the tortured railway yards. Of a sudden, a great spiral of smoke billowed up in ever ascending folds to our 14,000-foot level! The flak held back as we moved in to make our drop. Our group effort was like kicking a dead giant because he still quivered. Even so, we didn't kick very hard.

Our deputy lead, the first ship to take over in the event the lead was knocked out, was carrying an inexperienced bombardier. He became confused, and instead of waiting to drop on the lead, he hit his bomb release when he thought he was on target. Most of our bombardiers, watching for the drop, hit their switches on his signal. Larry held. It was an excruciating delay as bombs from practically the entire formation whistled down to smash into a section of the city bordering the railway yards. But in seconds bombs sprayed from the lead ship. Our plane and one other sent our loads down with him.

Only seconds; but a bomber traveling at 180 miles an hour covers a lot of territory. How much good—or bad— our group did that day was buried in the overall headlines Stateside that screamed: FIRST BIG DOUBLE STAB MADE BY FORTS, LIBS.

Our mission was far from over. Ahead was the biggest flak bed we had yet encountered.

This was a repetition of the black poppy field over Hamm. Only this one, equally concentrated, was spread for miles along our course. Off and on, we rode above, below, and through flak until it seemed almost a normal part of the scenery. Yet no planes seemed to be hurting. The tiny black clouds seemed no more harmful than the occasional wisp of white encountered on a clear day. Only God knows how or why the bombers made it through, but suddenly the air was clear. We followed another group northwest toward the southern coast of Belgium. The group ahead seemed a bit south of course, but we had no alternative except to follow. Other groups were squeezing in from the sides, all heading home.

Finally we could see the reflected glow on the North Sea of the sun which was rapidly settling behind the haze over England. Only 180 miles to home. It looked like clear sailing. But for some weird reason, our lead had chosen to come over Lille, in France. They were ready for us.

Hell shattered the shadowed city where it seemed a gun

was twinkling on every street corner. The flak was big and black. But there was more than the normal load of anti-aircraft fire. Much of the stuff coming up had no marking charge. You could see the yellow balls bursting out front amid the usual hummocked field of black puffs with their lethal centers. But nothing remained after the flash. Despite the fresh confidence inspired by the fine airplane we rode, I began to feel uncomfortable. Much as we hated them, the normal flak bursts had become part of the game. As always, as in all things, the unknown factor created apprehension we had known before coming away from Hamm. Yet, from the size of the aerial flashes, we knew it was small stuff. But there was so much of it! The air was too crowded.

"There's a '24 going down in the group to the right," Cox came through on the interphone as though to confirm the threat of too many guns. "A chute is hung up on one of the other planes."

I stole a quick, fearful glance across to Jack's window. There I could see it. A ship with number two engine feathered had picked up the parachute of some poor devil who had bailed out higher up. It was a sickening sight even though we were too far away to see the face of the doomed airman. Almost within fly rod's reach of the men in the Liberator, the man dragged the air on his twin tether was as good as dead. We knew it; everybody who could see his predicament knew it. Worse, the man knew it.

But now our formation was taking violent evasive action. It became tattered and scattered as we banked among the bursts trying to find an alley of open air. However, the guns had had a chance to practice on the group which preceded us. They had our altitude and air speed. Our '24 was bucking badly to the explosions; we were getting hits!

"Number two is losing oil—bad!" Renfro had spotted it. I looked.

In trying to keep some semblance of formation despite the wild gyrations of our squadron and the rough, explosion wracked air, I hadn't noticed the leaking engine. But it was in trouble, bad trouble. Oil was pouring from a leak that bubbled from one of the lines behind the prop before it was churned into spray and smoke behind the engine. I made a quick check of the pressure gauge; it was already down, down dangerously.

I hit number two feathering button and watched the three blades come slowly slicing into the wind. We had caught it in time; otherwise the oil-starved Pratt would soon have frozen to a standstill with the blades almost flat to the air, a real drag.

Even as I reached for the trim tab adjustment to lift the crippled wing, the right rudder suddenly went dead. My foot shot to the floor as though there was no rudder, and the plane yawed right. I planted both feet on the left rudder and motioned to Jack to help. To further aid in keeping the wing up, I flicked on the auto-pilot. It gave a little relief to my aching arms and legs.

Still the Liberator bucked to the concussion. There were three bad bursts; we could hear them and we could feel them. It was the ones you could not see that hurt. And, we were getting hurt! Two large holes in the bomb bay attested to one burst that had found us. Still the right rudder would not respond; I was certain that a cable had been severed. I forced the Liberator to the left, away from the lead ship in the box, so that we wouldn't take anyone else with us if we blew.

We began to lose altitude with the loss in power. I eased the throttles up a fraction to hold our relative position. Automatically my eyes took a fast photograph of the instrument panel. They caught on the number four cylinder-head temperature. It was dead! I hit the feathering button. As the blades turned their cutting edge into the air, pressure came back to the right rudder. It had been the drag of the props on the dead engine plus the trim which took all the left rudder and aileron pressure. With an engine feathered on each side, controls returned to nearly normal, but we were dropping fast. Beneath us, coastal batteries of all sizes were roughing up the air. Our altimeter read 13,000 feet.

We had been taught in training that the Pratt-Whitneys

should not be held at takeoff manifold pressure, forty-nine inches, for more than five minutes. Beyond that, their life expectancy was nil. We had also been told that the B-24 would not maintain altitude on two engines. These thoughts were stark in my memory as I glanced at the dead prop on each wing. The nearest friendly airfield was eighty miles away.

I moved the two remaining engines up to 49 inches. And I locked the throttles in place. As far as I was concerned, they would stay there until the engines blew to hell, they took us across the English Channel, or I had to play them into a forced landing in the water. In the same moment, I was on the interphone.

"Rowland, don't break radio silence, but start firing flares for fighter cover. We don't have far to go, but we don't want any strange company." The radio man was ready with his flare gun to blast the oversized shotgun shells loaded with green light through the opening over the flight deck. "Now, all of you—we're in trouble. Keep your chutes handy. And start dumping everything over the side that will move . . . radios, flak vests, guns, ammunition—anything!"

After firing his flares, Rowland went back to his radios to send out an SOS over regular channels. Outside, firing had stopped. We were well out over the water, but we were descending toward it much too fast for comfort. Unknown to us, two P-38's had picked up our signals and were mothering our trail.

Meanwhile, Sanders had been busy checking. He found where wires to number four had been severed by flak and busied himself trying to make a temporary splice. He had already cleared everything that wasn't bolted down from the flight deck. Back in the waist, Cox, Reichert, and Renfro were busy dumping anything that would move over the side. Schow had left his tail turret to help. He finally called, "There isn't even a slip of paper back here!"

Rauscher had pointed me toward the closest field, one near the mouth of the Thames River, east of London. We were descending on a visual course directly toward it.

While the men were busy unloading the airplane, my mind was revving in time with the propellers. I had a big decision to make, and time for making it was running out. These kids of mine had not asked one question although their thoughts, too, must have been racing. Finally, I had my answer, and I wasn't at all sure it was a good one.

I was in love with this airplane, and I didn't want to lose her. There was a fair chance of getting her down in one piece. But on two engines there was only one chance. Consequently, I would order all the crew but Emerson to bail out as soon as we were over open land. Jack could have his choice—bail or ride her in with me. That is, this would be my plan if we made it to the mainland. Even then, it would have to be a one try, straight-in approach on the nearest runway to our heading. We couldn't maneuver much on two engines. And we wouldn't get a second try.

Things were looking better. The altimeter was dropping more slowly as we settled into the heavier air. Finally, the drop was almost imperceptible. Then the needle settled right on 6,000 feet! We were still on two; but we were flying! The smog drifting out from London wasn't inviting, but the dull haze only partly obscured the land ahead.

Then I felt Bill Sanders' hand on my shoulder.

As usual, Bill had been busy. On this particular flight, his energy had undoubtedly saved his life. For, back when the flak was flying, he had made his first check to look for trouble when number four failed. Rowland took over the top turret while Bill was busy. When he re-entered the turret, he ducked momentarily to reach for his oxygen mask. As he sat upright, he was greeted by a large hole in the plexiglas right in line with his head.

Without knowing it at the time Schow had picked up a piece of flak which zipped through his flying suit and ended up against his underwear. But these were incidental to the main problem.

"Sir," Sanders said, "I think there's a chance that number four will work. I made a splice that may do it."

At this point, I didn't need any urging. I touched the

prop governor and eased the blades back into the wind. The propeller started to windmill as three pairs of eyes glued to the oil pressure. It was starting to rise! I urged the prop ahead and watched the instruments respond as though nothing had ever happened. Bill's grin was cutting both sides of his helmet. We watched a few minutes more, finding it hard to believe, finally convinced. I matched the three throttles at normal cruise and squeezed my throat mike.

"We're back on three. How would you characters like to go home?" The exact answers were lost in a blur of agreement that jarred my ear drums.

16

Clear skies beamed ahead, a respite beyond
For each living still, a battle unwon;
For those who in glory had severed their bond
Winged with their course set due West with the sun.
> *From "First Time to the Target"*

Rauscher gave me a heading for the base of the 44th.
Our radio compass was out, and we slid over the haze on
a course almost due north by magnetic compass. It was a
wonderful feeling to have sufficient power again. And with
the airplane lightened, she was flying nicely on three.
Number one and number three, which had exceeded everything ever expected of them, showed no visible signs
of their recent torture. All instruments registered okay. As
though to make up for her recent transgressions, the B-24
handled like the lady she was. I grabbed another 1,000
feet on the way home to give us an extra measure of security in the event the lady relented. It looked dark down
through the haze as we approached home base on Rowland's bearings taken from the field. But we still had some
sun at 7,000 feet.

"We'd better check the tires before we go down," I
suggested to Jack, throttling back so that he could lower
the gear. "You fellows back there take a good look," I
called as the landing apparatus bumped into position. Jack

and I paid special attention to the hydraulic pressure as the mechanism was in operation. All reports were affirmative, and we called for landing instructions.

"You'll have to stay up there a while," the tower informed us. "We have an airplane on the main runway with a broken nose wheel. We'll have it cleared for you shortly."

This was no good, not in our situation.

"We can't stay up here," I called. "We're on three now, and we don't know how long we will have them. We were on two."

There was a considerable delay, then the tower came back.

"We have you cleared to use the short runway. Cut it as close as you can; you don't have much room. You're clear to land when ready."

The "short runway" was just that. We had never used it before. In fact, we had never seen anybody use it. Just over 5,000 feet, it was a marginal landing strip for Liberator bombers. Nevertheless, there was sufficient length for landing if you didn't press your luck too hard. Lady Luck had been nice to us; we didn't want to offend her. I swung wide for a good look before settling in on my approach. We might not get a second opportunity on three engines.

I had never paid any attention to the strip before. It had a slight rise in the center where it crossed the main runway. We eased onto the concrete well within the first third of the paved distance. Actually, when I saw lights across the runway, I tipped the brake pedals. Jack, who sat considerably higher, hollered across at me.

"You've got lots of room!"

Even as he called out, I, too, could see that we had plenty of runway left over the rise as we rolled across the main strip. This would be important to both of us at the critique the next day. Then it was time to start pumping the brakes to bring the bomber down on her haunches. As usual, I tipped them tentatively, to give the tires the feel of the concrete before tormenting the brake drums in earnest. Nothing! There was no feel to the brakes at all!

Jack sensed I was in trouble when there was no familiar buck at the brakes. He joined me in standing against the brakes with everything we could muster while crushing the wheels into our stomachs. Nothing! Absolutely nothing except a dreadful sinking sensation that our really big trouble was ahead of us rather than behind. The touch of brakes earlier had slowed us a bit, so that there was no rudder control remaining, and we were headed for a rough ride.

A first glance to where we were headed brought some relief. It was an open field, with about a 20 percent upgrade, and it didn't look too rough—if it wasn't muddy. Then, out of the dusk loomed a ditch! It was a big one, right across our intended path. Not more than a hundred yards off the end of the concrete!

If we hit that head-on, something most unpleasant was apt to happen. Yet, with no brakes and no rudders we had no choice. In that last instant as we left the runway, I hit number one throttle full blast. There was no time for a ground loop, but the lady started to respond. She turned her head just enough to take the impact on her left shoulder as we hit the ditch. There was a great, searing crash, a heavy jolt—then nothing.

In practice, we could clear an airplane in eleven seconds. In something under that, the entire crew was well out away from the airplane in a fan on her less damaged side. I flipped a few switches and followed Jack out the top hatch and down the nose.

It was a short jump to the ground. The nose wheel had been completely sheared off and lay in pieces in the ditch. She lay on her left side, one wing touching the ground outboard of the number one propeller which had plowed into the soft earth. The feathered propeller on number two just cleared the ground. The ditch had whipped her partly around, warping her fuselage badly, but her right wing was still held aloft, like the supplicating stretch of a gunshot pigeon's wing still attached to a shattered body. She had a faint odor of hot oil and gasoline about her, and a thin streamer of smoke drifting up from her crushed number one.

I hoped that I counted right as each of the crew grabbed my hand in turn. Then the firemen and medics mingled with us. Schow was suffering from shock and Davis had cut himself slightly on a brace in the bomb bay. That was the limit of our injuries.

But the airplane was finished. I wandered back to her. Voices yelled, "Get away from her! She might go up!" I ignored them. She wouldn't hurt me. This wonderful, wonderful airplane wouldn't hurt me. She was dead. She was dead and I had only known her for a part of a day. Every good feeling I had about flying was tied up in her; she was everything a bomber pilot could want. I knew there was nothing I could have done to prevent her finish under the circumstances. But this didn't ease the pain. Oh, maybe if I hadn't touched the brakes to use up the pressure in the accumulators, I might have held her back when the right time came. But we had checked, both Jack and I, and her hydraulic system read right. Something had let go. Maybe a flak-weakened line had let go after we checked her upstairs.

A colonel came over to me. I don't remember who it was, because I couldn't see so good. Maybe he noticed that I couldn't see so good, because he put his hand on my shoulder.

"Don't let this bother you, Schuyler," he said kindly. "It wasn't your fault; we should have had that ditch filled."

He had missed the point of my grief. I knew damned well it wasn't my fault. My boys were all okay. I wasn't bothered about the accident. But, lying battered and smashed in front of me was the personification of every effort I had put into my training and my war. I had hated the Liberator only to love her. I had been afraid, only to regain whatever measure of confidence is permitted a soldier, because of this airplane. Since *Sweet Eloise*, this unnamed creature had been the first to claim whatever it was I had to offer. And she had come to me when I needed her most. She had made herself available after I had become a soldier. I mumbled something back to the colonel.

"It's not that; she was *our* airplane."

So you get sentimental. And if somebody doesn't respect your tender feelings, you get mad. Both Jack and I got damned mad at the critique the next day.

We were flying so often that we seldom had time for critiques, the chance to go over a mission and discover too late the mistakes that can prove so costly. It was the weather that set this one up.

After an episode, in varying forms, of our experience of the day before, it was customary to give the crew a couple of days off to get their collective stomach back in place. However, when we checked the bulletin board after our crackup, we were listed for the next day's mission. It would have been all right with us but for one reason. Sergeant Schow wouldn't be able to go with us because the medics didn't want him to go back out so soon. We felt better going out as a complete crew. So we didn't mind the delay when the weather moved in. Anyway, critiques were interesting. Especially this one.

It was about the middle of the session when the major holding the critique mentioned the accident. He was real damned polite; he didn't mention any names.

"We are not blaming the pilot, because we should have had that ditch filled. However, had he landed farther up the runway, he might have been able to save the ship."

Why, the dirty son of a bitch! I was on my feet, fast. If he was trying to protect me by not mentioning names, I didn't need any protection. But this *was* the army. Without being recognized by the major, I was on my way.

"Sir, I was the pilot of that airplane! I landed well within the first third of the runway. That's a good landing anywhere!"

"Well, you may have *thought* you were on the first third of the runway," the son of a bitch simpered, "but I was watching from the tower. And I could see the smoke from your tires when you landed."

"You were in the tower, a mile away, and you are telling *me* where I landed?'' I countered, visions of a court-martial flitting through my blind range. "It was almost dark! You probably saw the smoke from my tires when I made the first application of brakes. I must have still had some pressure in my accumulators.''

"Lieutenant, I *know* where you landed,'' the s.o.b. delivered with finality.

I had about shot my wad. Anyway, I was afraid to trust myself to say anything further. I just stood there in mute defiance. But Jack, who was probably the least likely guy in the 8th Air Force to get mad at anybody, jumped to his feet.

"Major,'' he said, his face flaming. "I was the co-pilot on that airplane. The landing was just as Lieutenant Schuyler said it was.''

It was obvious to everyone that both Jack and I were embarrassed in addition to being furious. It was the major's turn to look uncomfortable. He mumbled something about not blaming us for *thinking* we landed where were claimed and took off on another subject. There was nothing left for us to do but sit down. I was wishing the major and I could be civilians for about fifteen minutes.

There was a notice for Jack and me to report to squadron headquarters after the critique. The papers had come through on our promotions, and our signatures were needed. "It should only be a matter of a few days now,'' we were told. Whatever we signed ended up in somebody's waste basket.

The bulletin board notified us that we were up for the next day's mission. After dinner, I wrote my last letter to Eloise from England and hit the sack.

17

We climb once more the pinnacle of hope
With fingers desperate, and try to cling
On holds of faith, as spirits searching, grope
To find the next step that we pray will bring
Us conquest of the summit; for even now our lofty gain
Gives a glimpse of promise that our effort has not been
  in vain.

From "Hope"

Back in the States, our people were getting nervous. Letters from Europe came through with spasmodic frequency. Anyway, there wasn't much you could get by the censors about your real activities even if you were tempted to violate security. The home front had to go by what they read in the newspapers.

The news looked good as newspaper stories go. We were winning. But for every family with a member flying out of the European Theater of Operations, these were uncertain days. About our double raid of April 27, headlines proclaimed:

"3,000 PLANES IN RECORD CHANNEL SHUTTLE; 13TH DAY
OF MASSIVE ONSLAUGHT ON ATLANTIC WALL
FOLLOWS RAF SMASH."

American air forces in Britain struck their heaviest blow of the war yesterday. For the first time in history, two major fleets of heavy bombers went out from ETO bases to Nazi targets on the Continent, two big forces of Marauders and Havocs lashed at objectives in France and Belgium, and all through the day of unending blitz fighters and dive-bombers by the hundreds thundered against Hitler's Atlantic Wall.

What the newspapers could not tell the families of our crew was that we had flown seven missions in those thirteen days of "massive assault." But they knew we were in the middle of it, and they could only morbidly surmise that the brave headlines had their price.

Maybe it was fortunate that security held us to report only casual happenings. We might have been tempted to tell of the war as we knew it—of the thousands of little personal wars that couldn't make the headlines. Yet it was tough to find something to write home about. You had to build up mundane little things and make them sound important so that the folks wouldn't worry. Eloise and I had a little code which would give her some idea of what was happening. We worked through an intermediary named Pete.

Pete was actually a little stuffed doll, shaped somewhat like a gingerbread man with cotton stuffing in a pink exterior. About ten inches long, Pete was properly equipped with a seat-pack parachute with ribbon straps. His chute was packed with Friendship Garden sachet, a frequent gift to Eloise from me on special occasions. Button eyes completed the absurd likeness to an airman. Pete had been given to me by Eloise before I left the States, and his name was chosen for a purpose.

In my letters home, I could refer to Pete as a third person in casual references that gave Eloise a hint of what was happening. He was my pseudo personality, and it was unlikely that his activities would mean much to a German if one of my letters was intercepted.

For example, in one of my last letters home, I had this

to say about my little friend. "Pete is sitting here in the chair looking very button-eyed. Guess he's kind of tired; they got him up very early this morning and we went to breakfast together." Only Eloise knew who Pete was, and she knew if we "went to breakfast together" that I flew the mission for the day. She could fill in the details from the newspaper. So we had our little system of communications that could harm no one, but it brought her closer to my activities without violating security.

Pete had two other functions.

A whiff of his Friendship Garden could quickly take me back to some of the wonderful experiences my bride and I had shared as she took the circuit as a cadet wife. Like the graduation party in Indiana as we held hands in the shadows thrown by moonlight to the orchestra's interpretation of "The Way You Look Tonight." We had just discovered for certain that she was pregnant. This put the seal of approval on the man-and-wife relationship we shared. And for me there was a warm pride that our physical union was productive. For her there was that special bloom of happiness which accentuates the beauty of any woman carrying her first child. The sachet could quickly bring back the memory of one night when I sneaked into her forbidden quarters at Maxwell Field when we met for the first time after nearly three months separation.

Some men had their silk stockings, a garter, maybe a pressed flower. To a man we would vehemently deny any trace of superstition. Yet there were probably few who did not carry some symbol of religion, love, or pagan charm just to be on the safe side of sentimentality. As a "just in case" my Roman Catholic cousin in Philadelphia had impressed upon me a St. Christopher medal that had a special place in my wallet. Despite all this occult frivolity, these charms and amulets came to have a special meaning about as ethereal as their supposed powers.

It had become habit to tuck Pete inside my shirt as a regular preparation for the mission before leaving my hut. He was then promptly forgotten in the assumption that he would perform whatever mystic powers he possessed. Actually, he was just a bit of home, a symbol, and a rapidly dirtying fetish at that. So I thought. Yet it was on the trip home from Hamm that I suddenly realized that I had forgotten to bring him along. I remember clapping my hand to my jacket as a faint chill crept up my spine. Then I remembered that I wasn't superstitious and promptly forgot about the doll. Funny that I still remember clapping my hand to my jacket. Pete didn't miss another trip.

He went along on April 29, 1944—to Berlin.

When the word had come through increasing a tour of duty from twenty-five to thirty-five missions, later reduced to thirty, it had pretty well knocked out any hope we had of finishing. This gnawing fear of the inevitable was further heightened by the heavy losses our group had sustained. Yet, getting through the double trip on the twenty-seventh had somewhat restored our confidence. Even more than the experience, the fact that we had been given a relatively new airplane for our last mission helped. We knew, too, what a B-24 could take and what it could do. But our *new* airplane would fly no more. I had no idea what was lined up for us on the next trip. Rumors had been flying that we would soon have plenty of new airplanes. The old olive drab was being abandoned for the natural silver, and these sleek new ships were beginning to show up more and more in the various groups we saw over England and the continent.

18

Then bomb bays belched forth from bowels swelled with
*   hate:*
Dripping in torrents their droplets of dread;
Drowning pitiful prayers pleading too late;
As even the only God bowed His head.
*   From "First Time to the Target"*

There was a murmur through the briefing room as the
pointer settled on Berlin the morning of the twenty-ninth.
But the usual moan in unison was lacking as though the
men could not squeeze any levity out of the situation. As
a group, we were tired. Implications of the long haul, after
days of bombing missions every time the weather permitted, crushed in on us, smothered us.

Berlin was always a rough one. This was the symbol of
German's might. In an ideological effort, symbols are important. You protect them with your life. There were still
plenty of German fliers willing to die for Berlin for ideological reasons. There were plenty more who had lost their
grasp on symbols but flew and fought as exquisite machines that were manufactured out of the best parts available. Germany's best was plenty good enough. She had
been hurt, badly. But like any creature that has been mor-
tally wounded, she was still capable of fighting like hell.

This we knew when the pointer settled on Berlin.

"You can expect heavy fighter opposition," we were told. "The Luftwaffe has been unusually quiet for the past week, and we expect plenty of trouble today. You will have fighter cover much of the way, but you know they can't stick around long. Keep your formation tight so that the German fighters can't get through. We have tried to route you around the worst flak, but it will be rough over Berlin."

The weather would provide some clouds, but it was expected to be broken enough for good bombing. Our plane was assigned to the lead squadron. We would be flying left wing in the second element. It would be another busy day for Jack. Waning night was cool and starlit as we rode the truck to the dispersal area. Sanders had checked over the airplane, and his report was encouraging.

"She's not quite the airplane that the last one was, but she's a good one."

The enlisted men were always alert to my arrival at the airplane. This was one of the few disciplines I had imposed on them. In this manner, we could quickly go over the necessary inspection and reports so that all of us knew about what to expect from our airplane. They had been briefed, and we knew what we were in for together. Our crew was complete this morning. This was the way we had started on our first mission which now seemed so long ago. This was the way we wanted to end our war, win or lose.

There was a kind of pathetic quality to the group as the men lined up in front of the airplane. They looked like half-dressed Eskimos, too small for the whale-long fuselage behind them. It was not until we were close enough in the usual half-light, and I could see their faces, that they became people. These youngsters who had started together were no longer youngsters. They were men. Even Bill Sanders' grin, which had survived the ages of our indoctrination into manhood, had a different quality. It was still genuine, but drawn, and lined with the tremendous sense of responsibility that he had discovered his job really entailed. Bill knew much of what it would take to get this B-24 to Berlin—and back.

Cox and Reichert looked just a little old for their years, much older than they had been only twenty-one days before on our lighthearted try for our first.

Maybe George Renfro showed it most. He was the youngest in years, and his transition to a level of manhood that we now all shared had been the greatest jump. He had been a frustrated belly gunner until he saw what came up from the ground toward this exposed part of the Liberator's navel. Then he had wanted no part of it. I remembered the first chance I gave him to get ready in the event that something happened to Reichert and I needed George in the ball turret. Several of us were walking across the barracks area right after an announcement that we would have a day off. It was after our first rough one to Bernberg.

"This will give you a chance to practice in the belly turret," I told George, jerking my thumb toward the area where a working model had been set up for the purpose. "Give it an hour tomorrow."

Renfro looked at me in utter disbelief, then broke out in his regular Texas grin.

"In a pig's ass, I will!"

We were considerably more than whispering distance apart, and George's exclamation covered quite an area. I walked closer.

"George, old boy, I know just how you meant that. But if the colonel should have been walking by just then, you would have made us both look pretty bad." Poor George's face dropped to his shoe strings. "Now, you get *two* hours in the belly turret." He was apologetic to the point that it was my turn to be embarrassed.

That was the closest I ever came to having to discipline any of the men. And that was a complete bust. Headquarters crossed us up and we were scheduled for the mission the following day. George never did get his time in the ball turret. Looking at him this day of the Berlin mission, I was confident that he would find a way to do whatever job was demanded of him.

Schow was in love with his guns. He showed the strain of recent weeks, but there was a deadly earnestness in his demeanor whenever he was in the proximity of his twin fifties. He made me feel as though nothing could possibly get through Sergeant Harry J. It was a good feeling. Rowland, imperturbable as ever, was probably the least affected. Until the bad bust of two days before, he had not had to concern himself with other than his radios. Yet even he reflected the strain of the pace.

Living together, the four of us with lieutenant's bars didn't notice the changes among ourselves as much. We lived our fears and concerns as a part of our daily association. However, the wounds were as deep. They were just not as noticeable.

Number ten. If we got to the action, this would give us an oak-leaf cluster on our air medals except for the two who had missed one mission. It was merely a thought in passing. It would take six clusters to buy a ticket home. And, at this point, the price seemed much too high and unattainable.

Automatically I eased the engines into action in the knowledge that the crew chief had already made over sixty checks of the airplane. But, I watched the oil pressure move between the green lines daubed in at sixty and eighty pounds as though my first instructor was looking over my shoulder. Cylinder head temperature on each engine climbed slowly toward the max of 205°C; oil temperature moving into the proper range above 60°C; manifold pressure; fuel pressure; prop governor; magnetoes; generators; vacuum pumps; de-icers; and the countless other mechanical marvels needed to get this chunk of machinery airborne and to keep her there. It's a long way to Berlin—and back.

Down the taxi strip and a quick check of each engine individually at 1600 rpm's. Flaps down, gear locked, props in full low pitch, mixture full rich, cowl flaps closed. Turn into position for takeoff as soon as the ship ahead is airborne. Brakes full on, throttles slowly ahead until each horse had the bit in its teeth. Turn 'em loose! And you feel the power dragging at the wings with a positive pull, and you know you have another good airplane. Maybe not quite as tight as the last, but good. The airspeed needle keeps gaining on 120 mph with lots of runway left. You feel for lift, find it, and urge her off the concrete at 120. Level a bit until you have packed more air under your wings to gain flying speed, then up toward the twin tail a few hundred yards ahead of you.

Strung out like a flock of pelicans, ugly and awkward on the ground but ever so graceful in the air, the formation heads out over the North Sea.

"Okay to check guns," you call, and the ship shuddered as ten 50's talk. Gradually the gaps close until the string of bombers has bunched into three tight units headed for a target over five hundred miles away. This is the way you go to Berlin; and Berlin is *always* a rough one.

Royal Air Force Lancasters had pasted a major German air base repair depot at Kjeller, eleven miles outside the Nazi held Norwegian capital of Oslo during the night. Mosquitoes had hit Hamburg without loss during the dark hours. Diversionary raids were being staged by light bombers near Rennes in northern France this day. Down south five hundred Forts and Libs were smashing at the submarine pens and the port of Toulon on the French Mediterranean coast with a side trip to Genoa. All of this was designed to inflict the maximum damage, and ostensibly, to take some of the pressure off us. But the Luftwaffe would be waiting. There was this matter of the symbol.

Although much of the activity in this phase of the air war was to knock out the German capability to produce aircraft and aircraft parts, we knew that the job was far from complete. Consequently, the belt of fighter bases, lined north and south of Hanover halfway between Berlin and the west border of German proper, was certain to have plenty of power remaining. The fact that it had not been used on recent days was an ominous indication that the Sunday punch might be reserved for this Saturday.

As we sailed in across the Zuider Zee, flak fields ahead

were little more than nuisance notice of the potential trouble ahead. On each side of us there were other groups absorbing some of the flak batteries' attention, and one group at a lower altitude on the left lost a ship before we had covered much of the Dutch sky. Then we crossed the German border just north of Osnabruk. Flak was spotty—not too hard to dodge. Groups ahead helped provide a route through the stuff. And, we knew the slower B-17's had used up some of the ground ammunition on their way in ahead of us. Some fighters overhead, friendly fellows cutting contrails back and forth in a protective web that made you feel good. Then Larry Davis cut in on the interphone.

"Fighters! A whole swarm of them!" I didn't see them at once. Larry pinpointed them. "Straight ahead, low at twelve o'clock!"

Then I saw them. I took a deep breath. Coming up at us like a swarm of bees was a literal swarm of at least forty German fighters. And they were headed directly at our formation! Like specks at first, in almost an instant they materialized into wings and engines.

"Give it to them," I hollered, and held tight. Trying to move in this mess would invite collision. They were packed and stacked!

Then there was a hellish roar as everything became a confusion of sound and motion. Like entering a tunnel with the window open on a train, dust, noise, and debris became indistinguishable. Right over my windshield a German fighter came apart in a glimpse of flame and junk. That was Larry's. My impression was little more than a flash.

From the top turret, Sanders cut the tip from the wing of a Messerschmitt 109. As it sloughed toward the ground, Schow gave it a burst. Then another 109 came into Harry's sights and he kept the triggers down. The fighter started an abrupt climb, stalled, and disappeared down out of sight.

A B-24 that had been lagging at seven o'clock drew in close at five o'clock just as a German came through. The fighter smashed head-on into the big one right at the nose turret and both planes exploded in a ball of flame.

Then it was over. Just like that. But back through the formations behind us the Germans barreled with reckless abandon. Airplanes were going down in every direction, the cripples staggering out of formation, clinging to life—then blowing up or fluttering down out of sight.

We had been caught with our fighters down. But now our single-engine friends moved in for the kill. The fight drifted behind. My instruments read right. We had made it through the fighter belt on the way in. Our incendiary load still hung quietly in the racks, waiting to see if we would make it to Berlin.

Berlin was visible long before we arrived.

In the greatest daylight raid of the war to that date, German's capital city was a mass of flames and explosions as we approached. And the maelstrom of churning guts, flame, smoke, and debris extended up to the level at which we went in. Although we sat four miles above the city, we soon became a part of the picture. It wasn't pretty. The air seemed filled with bombers, but each group was taking its own heading for its own particular part in this destruction. Each course was marked by a lane of flak from the hot guns below. Somehow, we went on. And then the bombs burst out of the bays like steel confetti and scattered with the wind on their Satanic way, down, down, down. . . . They twinkled back at us from far below as our bomb bay doors rumbled to close the rupture in our belly. Our job was done.

But it was a long way home. . . .

19

Who waits until the gun is jammed
To lend a prayer to his last chips,
Already is and has been damned—
Dies with that prayer upon his lips.
                    From "Faith"

Somehow, after you have dropped your bombs, you get the feeling that everything is all right. If your airplane is working as it should, it becomes more a matter of whether you have enough gasoline for the trip back. At least that is the feeling you have. After all, the Germans had their chance to stop you, and they failed. The game is over. Why should they bother with you now? You've dropped your load.

But down deep inside you know it isn't over. This is not a game. The Germans know that you will be back with another load if you are permitted to go home. They have plans for you. They want to punish you for what you did if they can. So they try.

Maybe there is no other good way out. Maybe that is why the lead plane took us over Brandenburg on the way out. So the Germans get another good crack at us with their flak guns. They have had plenty of practice this day.

The flak was heavy as we approached the outskirts of
· Brandenburg. We passed close to a formation of B-17's

136

headed our way. I couldn't help thinking that these poor bastards would still be up here flying after we were on the ground. Never before had I realized the impressive difference in air speed between the B-17 and the B-24. We passed them almost as though they were standing still. That got us to the flak faster.

Although it was heavy, we seemed to be getting by without incident. In fact, the stuff was thinning out. Then I noticed four bursts off our left wing, maybe a hundred yards out, and just below our level. Then four more, closer. Fascinated, I watched as four more burst just ahead of and below our left wing, possibly 30 yards away. I didn't see the next bursts. But I heard them. And our ship shook to the concussion. Immediately, number two prop ran away. The torque, as the propeller screamed up to over 3000 rpm, dragged at our wing, and I leaned into the rudder, then hit the feathering button. I needed time to survey the damage. We were hurt again—badly.

A check of the crew brought all good word from that quarter, but a hole in the cowling of number two gave visual evidence that we had caught plenty from the last volley of flak. The manifold pressure on number four was down badly. The supercharger had probably been knocked out. The engine was running smoothly, but it wouldn't do much more than carry its own weight at the over 20,000 feet we were indicating. I eased the throttles ahead a bit to take up some of the slack. Things were under control, but they weren't good. I decided to see what could be done with number two.

Except for that hole in cowling, I could see no other damage to the engine. Propeller governors, one of the few faults with the Pratts, were apt to go haywire with a sudden change in power. Perhaps there was something left in the number two. I nudged the prop blades into the wind and fed it some power. The engine responded well, and I brought it back into cruising throttle. It pounded like a constipated threshing machine. But it was running. I suspected that a cylinder had been knocked out.

Normally, we wouldn't have too much to worry about,

but we were still a long way from home. The disruption in power had dropped us back behind the formation. There was no chance of catching up. I personally called the lead ship.

"Red leader, we've got some problem back here. Can you slow it down a little?"

"We'll try," the answer came back, "but we can't cut it back much."

I knew he had to maintain formation speed. And it soon became evident that we couldn't keep up. There was no point in continuing the conversation and alerting any Germans listening in that we would soon be a sitting duck. We kept dropping back—slowly, inexorably. . . .

If we were hit in the wings as much as I feared, there was a good chance that we would be losing gasoline from the wing tanks. I called Sanders. He climbed down from his turret to check the gas supply.

His report confirmed my suspicions. There was a serious imbalance in the gasoline tanks to indicate that we were losing some somewhere. I asked Raucher for our estimated time of arrival in England. Some fast mental calculations convinced me that we were not going to make it home. If my figuring was right, the best we could hope for would be a ditching about halfway across the North Sea.

The crew couldn't help but be aware that I was concerned about the gas supply. But, I said nothing to let them in on my grim secret. Rauscher could suspect, and Sanders looked worried, but at that point I was the only one who had complete information. Even to make the North Sea, we would need to use all our altitude to stretch our glide as far as possible.

We were now so far back that I was no longer sure that we were following our own group. A short distance ahead of us another crippled Liberator was dragging toward home. And, on ahead of him there was another single B-24. I called Schow.

"Is there anything behind us?"

"No. We're all there is."

Even today, when I think back to those times of trouble, I am amazed at the performance of the entire crew. Not once did they ask a question. As though sensing the burdens that sat with me in the pilot's seat, they never added to them by asking questions that I could not or feared to answer. Always, they kept me informed of anything they thought I should know. But they did not probe into my troubled thoughts. This was one of their greatest contributions. They stood by their guns, the charts, the radios. In return, I tried to keep them posted.

"We are approaching the fighter belt. Keep your eyes open. If we can get past the fighters we might make it."

I couldn't make it sound too good. Everyone could feel the vibration of the sick engine, and it was obvious that we were alone. The conversations about the gasoline supply and Rauscher's estimated time of arrival certainly did not engender much optimism. Again it was Larry who altered us to fighters.

"Off to the left. They are hitting that group off to the left."

Well ahead, ten miles or more, we could see the action at about ten o'clock and at our level. I prayed that they wouldn't see us. But it didn't matter. Straight ahead there was another flock of fighters slicing through the group that I thought was the 44th. Bright twinkles of 20-mm cannon and the smoke of machine guns were visible even at this distance.

Directly ahead of us, the second cripple also saw them. Black blobs began to drop from the B-24. At first, I thought they were kicking loose some bombs which had become hung up. But then, the black blobs blossomed into parachutes. That crew wasn't going to stick around for the fun. I never did see what happened to the other single. Because, now all my attention was directed to the fighters.

There were eight of them! And had they elected to come at us singly, subsequent events might have been different. But they came straight on, strung out wing to wing, like a shallow string of beads. Focke Wulf 190's they were. And under other circumstances they would have been beautiful to watch. But I had only an instant to make my decision of how to deal with them.

Whether I was wise, foolhardy, or stupid is left to the interpretation of the individual reader. In the brief seconds left to decide, a thousand thoughts raced through my mind. One was paramount: We had come to fight. It never occurred to me to abandon the airplane, although our position was hopeless. I had a real affection for every man on that airplane, but I would not ask them to run away. Nevertheless, we were about to be blasted out of the sky. There was little chance that all of us would get out alive. I had nothing in my hands to fight with except the total airplane. So I used it.

"Get ready," I called. I, too, got ready. I didn't make my move until I saw the leading edges of the FW's start to smoke and yellow balls to pop around our wings. Then I dove straight for the middle of the string of beads! Either they would get out of the way or we would take a couple of them with us. In any event, they could not all aim their airplanes at us if they scattered.

They scattered.

All of our machine guns seemed to be going at once as FW's scrambled out of our way in every direction. I couldn't see the action, but from shouts over the interphone, two of them were badly hit and on their way down. So were we.

Deliberately, I held the nose of the bomber as straight down as I could manage. But, she was trimmed for level flight and wanted to come out of the dive. Jack saw my quivering arms and added his strength to keep the nose down. I wanted those fighters to think that they had us. The strategy worked on five out of the six remaining, but that one was destined to give us more trouble than all of the others combined. He didn't believe me.

That one German peeled off and came after us. I heard Jack shout under his oxygen mask as I felt the controls wrenched from me for an instant. Jack had seen him coming from his side and he rolled the bomber into the attack. Tracers cut by the left side of the fuselage as the tortured

Liberator responded. We kept the pressure on the elevators and the nose toward the ground as I watched the air speed pass the red line. Then it touched 290 which gave us somewhere around 400 mph at our altitude. I didn't know how much of this the battered bomber could take.

Down below I could see a solid cloud cover. It was our only refuge. But, in one of the frequent paradoxes of war, to gain them was also our undoing. Our precious altitude, needed to get us somewhere near home, whatever the consequences, was being used up in one desperate effort to escape the more obvious danger from the fighters. We would willingly have taken on this one eager beaver who stayed with us, but to change tactics would undoubtedly bring the other fighters in for the kill. We were committed.

Twice more on the way down the one fighter came in on us. And, twice more we turned in to him as the clouds neared. Then we were enveloped in the mist, safe for the moment from our pursuer.

In an instant, we were in serious trouble of an entirely different kind. The front surfaces of our cold airplane, dropping down from some 20,000 feet to this warm air layer of cloud at 5,000, were immediately swathed in ice. Only a tiny triangle, less than the size of a folded handkerchief, was clear in the lower right part of my windshield. The top turret and the nose turret caught the frigid coating simultaneously. However, I was on instruments in the clouds, anyway, and my visibility was no immediate problem. My worry of the moment was with the controls. They were sticking badly. As fast as I would kick the rudders free of ice and work the elevators, they would stiffen up again. It was the first B-24 I had ever flown without de-icer boots on the wings.

"We've got to get out of this stuff to get rid of this ice," I cautioned the gunners. "Get ready. I'm going on top."

I poked the bomber's nose above the cloud layer and leveled off. A few minutes to let the metal of the airplane assume somewhere near the outside temperature would do it. But our little friend upstairs was waiting.

"Go down! Go down!" came from several gun stations as the 190 bored in.

I thrust the wheel forward, keeping my eyes on the instruments.

"Get up! Get up!" came just as emphatically as the plea to go down.

Puzzled, I glanced out the clear side window. We were right over a German airfield. At the altitude they could knock us down with a rock. I lifted the '24 up a little, watching out the side to make sure we were riding in the clouds. I rolled the bomber to a heading ninety degrees of our course. Maybe we could shake the fighter. After a short time, I took the original heading again, trying to keep hidden. The controls fought me back on every move. Even more serious was the loss of function in the two gun turrets. I warned the crew, then eased into the clear air on top.

"Get down! Get down!" came over the interphone to the shuddering stutter of machine guns.

Well, if there was no other way, we would stay hidden and hope for the best. Anyway, the controls were beginning to work a bit more freely.

I had time to consider our position. It wasn't good. We had given up our precious altitude just to stay alive and to keep fighting, but the end was inevitable. It was not a question of trying to save the ship; it was doomed. The one big question was just how long to continue this running battle before admitting we were licked.

So far, I was certain that none of the men had been hurt. We were licking along at 160 indicated, at least headed for home, and at this altitude number four was doing its full share and number two was still pounding away. Siting above us was the enemy we had come to fight. If we could knock him down, our job would be done. Then we could go as far as the gasoline would allow and our war would be over. But I had no desire to engage the FW 190. None of us were likely to get home unless we could find the underground, but I couldn't see risking one life on the airplane for another crack at the fighter. I held course and altitude. Then fate took another hand.

The cloud cover, which had parted so conveniently over Berlin to permit precision bombing, had been solid at our lower altitude for many miles. Now it started to break. At first we just hit small holes, then larger one.

This situation was made to order for the fighter. He apparently spotted us crossing the small ponds of open air, and when we hit a big one he came in. His first attack came at 5 o'clock on the tail. Schow told me about it later:

"I started firing. The tracers bounced right off him. And then, I was just pressing triggers and nothing was happening. It was an instant before I could find the extend of the damage. A 20 mm had hit us in the right elevator. It blew my hydraulic unit on the floor, clipped off my left gun, cut my mike cord about an inch and a half from my throat, and generally took my plexiglas."

The tail gunner tried to fire his right gun manually, but it too was ruined. Schow went to the waist, where a fire had started, put on his chute, and told Sergeant Cox to relay the news to me since his mike was cut. Cox had already been on the interphone.

"We have a fire back here in the waist," he said calmly by way of information.

He put no more emphasis on it than he would for a fire in an ash tray. But, it had serious implications to me. It was not uncommon for gasoline to run down inside a wing, if a tank was punctured, and spill into the bomb bay. We had evidence that we were losing gasoline; if fumes picked up that fire in the waist, we could become one big bomb! Then I learned about Schow's trouble.

"We have another fire in the tail," the message read. The hydraulic system for the tail turret had been blown from the fuselage wall and the fluid was on fire.

Again the clouds gave us temporary relief as the fighter maneuvered for another pass. I tried to think of an answer. It was uncomplicated and the only thing I could think of at the time.

"Put them out."

As the gunners were working on the flames and throwing out burning flak vests, I called to Sanders and Reichert. Our time must be getting short.

"Reichert, you take over the top turret while Bill checks the gas again."

I sensed the exchange of positions behind me, then the clouds opened up again. Reichert had not had one chance to fire a gun. Lowering the ball turret would rob us of about five miles an hour in air speed and use up precious gasoline. Every time we had hit fighters, we hit trouble. But, now Walt had his chance. The 190 came up off our right side, and the twin 50's followed him all the way. Then they stopped as Walt pressed empty guns.

"How is everything back there?" I questioned after the wide pass.

"Out of ammunition up here," Walt called back. "I still can't see through the frost on this turret," Davis reported from up front. I knew Schow's guns were out. Only Renfro was in business at the left waist. "Everything's okay here." But the passes were mostly from the right. I suspected that the fighter was out of 20 mm's; we hadn't seen any on the last pass. His machine guns may have been empty. That might have been why he made his last pass wide. But we had only one gun out of ten operative at the moment. There was extra ammunition, but it would take time to get it to the guns. The clouds were about all gone. Then I felt Sanders' hand on my shoulder.

"We'd better get out of here, sir. We're down to fifty gallons!"

20

Down dropped the parachutes;
  The chutes dropped down.
Veterans and recruits,
  We all dropped down.
Down through the ether,
  With hardly a sound.
But ever descending,
  We dropped to the ground.
            From "Spirit Encumbered"

So—the time *had* come. You expected it, yet somehow it couldn't be you. I didn't know if the fires were out in back; but it didn't matter now. Only fifty gallons. A B-24 burned over 200 gallons an hour when it was working *right*. Fifteen minutes of flying time left at the most. At perhaps a ground speed close to our indicated 160, this would take us forty miles. I called Rauscher. We had been flying all over the sky trying to shake the fighter, but I knew Dale would be trying to follow us on his navigation charts.

"Where are we, Rausch?"

His answer came back quickly.

"We are either just over Holland or very close to it."

Forty miles. Enough to take us about halfway across Holland, perhaps to the Zuider Zee. Right into the flak batteries that could pick us off like we were indeed a flying boxcar at this altitude. It *was* time. I found another cloud, a big one.

"All right, now listen carefully. Bail out. Don't hesitate. Delay your jump below the clouds. Good luck. And God bless you. Acknowledge!"

"Roger, bombardier."

"Roger, navigator."

"Roger, waist . . ."

I grabbed Bill Sanders' hand, briefly. He had heard the order. Jack caught the movement and looked over, puzzled. Bomb doors were opening. He was on interplane frequency and hadn't heard. I jerked my thumb back. "Bail out." Our fingers caught in a fleeting farewell, and he turned to clap Rowland on the shoulder at his radio table. There was no hesitation, no question; they went. And as they went, I made my one final gesture.

". . . over Holland or very close to it," Rauscher had said. The long-defeated Dutch were still our allies. A B-24 Liberator bomber could cause a lot of damage when it hit. I started a 180-degree turn. Let her blow in Germany! I took a quick glance back through the fuselage. It was empty. It was the emptiest airplane I had ever seen! In that brief second, I felt as lonely as I had ever felt in my life. I flicked on the aileron switch of the automatic pilot, always set for emergency. As I rose hurriedly from my seat, I felt something grabbing at my waist. It was the cord to my heated suit.

Carefully I reached back and unplugged it so that the cord wouldn't break.

Then I was on the catwalk of the bomb bays, sat down, to roll out, forward into the clouds. The wind swept my legs back. I gathered my feet under me on the catwalk and dived headfirst through the opening. As I tumbled below and away from our airplane, I had the sensation we once had as kids when we would dive under a high waterfall to get to the recess behind it. Then I extended my arms, as I had been taught, to get into correct forward position before opening my chute. I was in no immediate hurry.

I had told the crew to delay their chute for a number of reasons. The Kraut was still hunting for us, and he might foul a chute accidentally in the clouds. Or, as some had been in the habit of doing, he might gun the men in their chutes. The less time we hung in the sky, the less time the Germans would have to get to our landing site. And we could spare a moment or two to slow down to the terminal velocity of a falling human body of about 120 miles per hour. *I* almost waited *too* long.

When in good position, I grabbed the ring on the harness of my back pack, pulled, and felt the snap. I braced for the shock, but nothing happened. I looked at my harness. The cable was still trailing from its sheath! When I pulled again, the cable came free. I clung to the ring. Somewhere I had heard that a good jumper does not lose his ring.

I wondered why I couldn't see or hear our airplane. Years later, Renfro said he saw it blow all to hell as he was coming down in his chute. The 190 did come in on Schow. Hanging helpless, Schow just waved. The German waved back. He had his kill—chalk up one more B-24.

Strung out behind me were the other parachutes, some still higher than mine. I reached for my leg straps, to free them so that I could take off when I hit. But the ground was coming at me. I braced with bent knees, hit, and somersaulted in approved fashion. Military chutes let you down hard. But I was okay.

Quickly I gathered my parachute and tried to hide it from possible spotting planes. Off to my left about a hundred yards was a farmhouse, and when the German woman on the porch saw me look her way, she went inside. The sun was now shining brightly. It was about 1 P.M. I squinted toward the western horizon. There were bombers still in view sailing serenely into the west. B-17's. For an instant, I felt lonely. I thought of home. They would worry when they got the word.

Then I suddenly realized that I was alive and well. I felt ridiculously happy. Like the night I ran down the hospital steps away from all that I loved most, I felt a serenity completely at odds with my situation.

I had crossed another horizon.

Index